HOOP CITY

BY

SCOTT BLUMENTHAL
AND
BRETT HODUS

www.scobre.com

Scobre Press Corporation
2255 Calle Clara
La Jolla, CA 92307

Scobre Press books may be purchased for educa-
tional, business or sales promotional use.

First Scobre edition published 2002.

Edited by Debra Ginsberg
Illustrated by Larry Salk
Cover Design by Michael Lynch

ISBN 0-9708992-1-1

www.scobre.com

To all the dreamers...

We at Scobre Press are proud to bring you another book in our "Dream Series." In case this is your first Scobre book, here's what we're all about. The goal of Scobre is to influence young people by entertaining them with books about athletes who act as role models. The moral dilemmas facing the athletes in a Scobre story run parallel to situations facing many young people today. After reading a Scobre book, our hope is that young people will be able to respond to adversity in their lives in the same heroic fashion as the athletes depicted in our books.

This book is about two fictional basketball players, Tony Hope and his brother Mike. To us and to everyone who reads this book, these guys are much more than just "made-up" ballplayers, they're examples of what it takes to dream big dreams and fight every day to make those dreams a reality. Their story of perseverance, determination and hard work is one we all could learn from.

We invite you now to come along with us, sit down, get comfortable, and read a book that will dare you to dream big dreams as well. Scobre dedicates this book to all the people who are chasing their own dreams. We're sure that the "Hope Brothers" will inspire you to reach for the stars.

Here's Tony and "Hoop City."

This book is dedicated to the
memory of our friend,
Andrew Sloan.
(10/18/77 -8/20/02)

Andrew was a basketball fan, a
great man, a better friend.
His family, his friends, and this
book will carry his legacy
forever.

Sloan, this is for you, bro.

CHAPTER ONE

FIFTEEN HOURS

"I'm on your wing, T. On your wing if you need me."

I always knew where my brother Mike was on the basketball court. "Right here, Tony!" Mike shouted, giving another enthusiastic wave. I slowed my dribble as I reached a faded yellow three-point arc, drawing the defense in closer.

Two defenders blocked my lane to the basket, futilely swiping for a steal. I dribbled as fast as I could in between and around them like a racecar weaving through traffic. A voice from beyond the court shouted at me, "Pass the ball, showboat!"

As he finished those words I picked up my dribble, watching Mike streak toward the basket unguarded. I lofted an alley-oop pass toward the side of the rim. The guys surrounding the court were silenced as Mike left his feet and glided toward the hoop. He grabbed the pass in mid-air, and in one effortless motion, tomahawked the basketball home. Amidst a sea of 'oohs' and 'aahs' I heard another voice from beyond the fence, "Get off that rim. You ain't Jordan yet!"

The rim rattled as Mike let go and landed firmly on his feet with the backboard shaking behind him. If I were that tired backboard I would have slept easy that night, knowing that Mike and I were leaving in the morning to attend the University of New York. In fact, everyone who ever played against us at "the Jungle" would sleep well that night. Every day, Harlem's future stars lined up for a chance to play here. And every day, they went home disappointed. Mike and I owned these courts. But with our senior season in the rear view mirror and the two of us heading off to college in the morning, tomorrow will be a different day. Tomorrow, someone else will actually have a chance to win.

They call these courts the Jungle because out here, you've got to fight to survive. This is where the best players in New York City develop, right here in Harlem, a place where life isn't always easy.

The usual crowd stood around the fence surrounding the Jungle during our last game before college. They shook the metal links when we dunked, when we made a shot or a great play. Their love for basketball was unfazed by time and circumstance. These one-time great players squandered college scholarships and NBA dreams for lives of drugs and crime. They were lost, sipping from bottles of beer, wondering where their dreams had gone.

Mike and I watched each other carefully, refusing to get trapped on the wrong side of the fence. We're fraternal twin brothers, born two minutes apart at Hoffman Medical

Center, just across the river from Yankee Stadium. We've been partners since before we could dribble straight.

My name is Tony Hope, but people around here call me "T." People say my brother and I are gonna play in the NBA someday. Tomorrow morning we leave for college, for the University of New York. Leaving this place is gonna be the greatest and saddest thing that's ever happened to me. I love Harlem. I just hate what it does to people.

After Mike's dunk, we shuffled back and got set defensively. I could hear the buzz from the sidelines. "Last game for the Hope boys, huh?" I bent my knees and pulled on my shorts, palms out, feet moving, ready for oncoming traffic. Mike slapped his hands onto the concrete and yelled, "One-nothing! Play some D now!"

I was guarding Bo Johnson, the skinny point guard whose jump shot never seemed to miss. He was dribbling casually down the court, using his body to separate me from the ball. Bo's biggest problem was that he couldn't dribble to his left. I slid over in anticipation of his only move.

Just as I thought, Bo faked to his left and tried to beat me to the hoop right. I was ready and waiting. I stepped into his dribbling lane and knocked the ball clean from his hands. Bo started to complain that he'd been fouled, but his whining was aimed at the back of my head. I was already off and running. Nothing stood between me and the basket.

Mike was trailing me on the fast break and there was no one else in sight. "Right behind you, T! Showtime!" I knew exactly what to do. I pretended to go in for the lay up, but instead of scoring, I bounced the ball high off the tattered backboard and waited for Mike to snatch it from the air. He soared to the hoop, this time grabbing the basketball with his right hand and slamming the orange pill ferociously. The crowd began shaking at the fence again, "Did you see that? He was three feet above the rim!"

Mike and I bumped chests as the ball bounced helplessly below us. We dared Bo Johnson to pick it up and try his luck again. "Perfect pass, T!" Mike grabbed me by the shirt, "Now how's anyone gonna stop us, bro?" I smiled from ear to ear, envisioning our future as clearly as I had a thousand times before in my head.

We went on to win that game, 11 - 3. After we scored the final point, Bo Johnson threw the ball at my chest. He was always a sore loser, "That's bull, man. Didn't we make a rule that you and your brother couldn't play together?"

Mike walked up to Bo confidently. He palmed Bo's tiny head as he spoke, "I don't remember that rule. Do you, T?"

"Nope, I don't remember that rule either." I threw the ball back to Bo, "Who's got next over here? The Hope brothers are all finished."

Mike and I stepped off the court together for the last time. We moved toward the wood bench outside of Vinny's Pizza. Xavier White walked toward us. "Been a great ride fellas. Make us proud." He shook our hands and walked away as quickly as he came. I looked up and noticed a small line forming in front of us. Old friends approached one by one to wish us luck, reminding us of our responsibility to them and to Harlem. These were the same guys we'd played with since we were kids, back when they used to call me "Shorty" and the only passing lanes I could see were in between the legs of my opponents.

We started to watch the next game, quietly realizing that while our world was changing, life in Harlem would remain the same. A gust of wind flung trash through the holes in the metal links that enclosed the courts. Thirty or forty players had short conversations while they leaned against the fence or sat on a nearby bench. Younger players bounced up and down, stretching their legs, each ready to prove that he was the next great one. Tomorrow, these same guys would still be watching and waiting. Music would blast the same way as it had since we were little. Only tomorrow, Mike and I wouldn't be there to hear it.

"You know, it's crazy saying goodbye. I've got to be honest, I don't want to leave this place." Mike stared off into space as a few more guys from the neighborhood passed by. "I wish they had a college in Harlem with a good hoops team, I'd play here in a second." Mike was nervous about leaving home. In eighteen years of life, we'd only left New York twice. Once to meet my great aunt Debra (who didn't remember us anyway), and the other time was when Mom saved up enough money to send us to basketball camp in Boston. Life had been simple up until now.

With college fifteen hours away, things were about to get much more complicated. For me, leaving home was something I looked forward to. Advancing closer to my NBA dream was all I ever thought about. For Mike though, things were more complex. Don't get me wrong, he loved basketball too.

He was the captain of our team, and arguably the best player in the state. He'd also been crowned prom king, earned varsity letters in three sports, teachers loved him, and he was the most popular kid in school. Every girl I knew would blush when Mike glanced her way. I guess it's his easy smile, or the confident way he carries himself. People in Harlem followed my brother the way they would a movie star. So when Mike told me he didn't want to leave, I understood.

I stared into the crowded street, watching a homeless man search for scraps of food in an overstuffed garbage can. I tried to ease Mike's worries, "We need this move. You think life is good now, just wait until we're wearing NBA uniforms." I smiled. "Don't worry. We'll come back someday."

Steam rose up from the concrete streets. The August heat had taken over like a virus. Mike walked over to a hot dog vendor who sat in a lawn chair holding a broken umbrella. He was wiping sweat from the top of his head with an old handkerchief. Mike paid the man a dollar, slapped him five, and ate the undercooked dog in two bites. He walked back toward me, mustard running off his bottom lip, "All I'm saying T, is don't forget where you came from. This is home. We've got one last night in a place we've spent our entire lives. Let's make it a night we'll remember." Mike spoke with a determined look in his eyes.

"What do you mean?" I'd seen that expression on my brother's face before. Like when we were eleven, and he convinced me to sneak out one night and shoot hoops in the middle of winter. He called it "an experiment of will power." As it turned out, our will was strong, but our bodies weren't. We both got so sick that we missed two weeks of school. And Mom punished us for two more weeks after that.

Or the time Tommy Hillson called me "stupid," and Mike promptly broke his nose with a left hook. The next day Tommy's dad called Mom, and we had to go over and apologize. That mistake grounded us for another two weeks. My brother had been getting me punished my whole life. Yeah, I'd seen that look before. It meant trouble.

Mike stared off into space and I repeated myself. "What do you mean? What are you gonna do?"

Mike grinned mischievously. "Relax, T, I'm just going to this party tonight. You should come."

I was never much for parties, "I don't know. I've gotta pack."

"Pack? Come on!" He pleaded with me. "Let loose a little, who knows, maybe you'll have some fun."

I had a hard time saying no to my brother, "Who's going?"

He paused. "Nick and Devon are picking me up - "

I cut him off. "I'm not going anywhere with those guys. You shouldn't either."

"All right Mr. Perfect, forget I said anything. I'm doing what I'm doing, you can come if you want." Mike bumped knuckles with me and walked away. Fifty yards later, he stopped. He wagged his finger at me, speaking sarcastically, "And make sure you're in bed by ten, Mister." Mike and I shared a laugh as he turned the corner for home.

I stayed to watch the last game of the day at the Jungle. I couldn't understand why he was going to a party with those two morons. Well, I wasn't going with him. That much was for sure.

It was five o'clock already and the sun was beginning to hide behind some of the taller buildings. I desperately wanted it to be morning. In just fifteen hours Mike and I would be sitting in our dorm room at UNY. I couldn't wait. I bounced up from my seat, ready to begin the next chapter of my life.

Four blocks later I approached our east Harlem apartment, 335 159th Street. Climbing eight flights of stairs every day helped strengthen my calves. The only guy I knew who could jump higher than the Hope brothers was Terry Jackson. He lived with his grandma on the twelfth floor. When I reached our place I pulled my keys from a pocket in my backpack and chipped a few pieces of red paint from our beat up door. Mom always complained to the landlord about the splintered wood, but he never fixed anything.

Mike beat me home by a few minutes. He and Mom were sitting on the couch watching television when I walked in. I bent over to drop Mom a kiss on my way to the kitchen. She always had a smile on her face when her boys were in the house. I grabbed an apple from the fridge and took a huge bite. My cheeks were stuffed when my brother made a stupid face at me. I almost spit a pile of apple onto the floor, but swallowed through my laughter.

I stared out the kitchen window, thinking about college. The streets had turned black. *The night was moving in.*

I was startled by a knock at the door.

Mike jumped up from the couch, expecting company. When he opened the door, Nick Cipro and Devon Jacox were standing there with backpacks on. Nick stood about six-foot-three inches tall and was well built. He had dropped out of high school a year earlier to work at his cousin's hardware store, but drinking and drugs had taken over his life. Devon was a scrawny guy who had a high pitched laugh like a hyena. He'd also dropped out of school. These were not the people I wanted hanging around my brother.

I half-heartedly slapped hands with Nick and Devon, biting my lip to stop myself from telling them to leave. I didn't want these guys in my house, kissing my mother's cheek and taking my brother off to some party. I knew that, while they had nothing to lose, Mike stood to lose everything.

The room seemed to stand still. Devon made a funny comment and Mom started laughing. He laughed along with her and his high-pitched cackle really started to get at me. My eyes locked onto Mike's. I slowly shook my head from side to side. I spoke to him without saying a word. "Stay here tonight, Mike. We'll talk about UNY, look through pictures and pack our stuff. Me and you tonight, Hope."

It was just a few moments before the guys began heading out of the apartment. Nick and Devon wondered why I wasn't coming out with them. I think I said that I wanted to get a good night's sleep before my big day tomorrow. The truth was, I wanted no part of their plans. Mike followed his 'friends' out. I slapped my brother's hand before he left.

I stared out the peephole, watching him disappear down the stairs. Mike even walked like a future all-star, chin up, smooth steps, never a change of pace. People claimed that when all was said and done, Mike would be the best to ever come out of Harlem. I always knew my brother was a better player than me. My job was easy. If he was open, I passed him the ball. If he was covered, I set a pick for him. If he took a bad shot, I battled for the rebound.

The telephone rang just as Mike disappeared down the stairs. I moved away from the door to answer.

The voice on the other end was panicked. "Tony, it's Lloyd. Where's Mike?"

Lloyd Bright was a friend of ours from school. "He just left with Nick and Devon. What's up?"

"I talked to Perry and he said that party was going to be crazy tonight."

"What do you mean, crazy?" I asked.

Lloyd was quick. "You know what I mean. The kind of party you go to if you're looking for trouble."

My heart jumped. "Well, what should I do?"

"I don't know, man. But if I were you, I'd get Mike out of there." Lloyd sounded serious.

"Where's the party?" I spoke while I changed into a pair of jeans.

"That's the problem, I'm not really sure. Perry says it's somewhere over by the high school." His clue was vague.

I hung up the phone and frantically laced up my sneakers. By leaving with Nick and Devon, Mike had taken a terrible shot. I had to get the rebound. "Mom, I'm going to meet Mike."

Mom responded from her bedroom. " I thought you said you were getting a good night's sleep."

"I will." I tried to hide any panic in my voice. "I gotta

go, Mom." *If I kept talking, I'd lose track of Mike.*

"All right, baby. Be home by eleven-thirty."

I left the apartment, locking the door behind me. My last night in Harlem was going to be a lot different than I'd imagined. I wanted to be in my bed, dreaming of NBA super stardom. I wanted to be resting my head on my pillow, picturing myself with a University of New York jersey on my back, throwing alley-oop passes to my brother. Instead, I was racing out of our building as fast as I could.

When I reached the bottom of the staircase I spotted the guys walking east toward the river. I followed them stealthily from a block behind. I'd keep my eye out from a distance.

The three of them walked a few blocks until they reached Jenkins Park, better known in Harlem as "the Park." This was where kids shot hoops before they earned an invite to the Jungle. I stopped for a second and remembered back when I played on these same beat up courts. The holes we'd cut out of the fence years ago to avoid the locked gates seemed to have shrunk in size. Or maybe I'd just gotten bigger. The rims still had no nets and on the far backboard, the letters 'LW' were written in bright blue. I knew those initials, Lamar Williams, Harlem's greatest player. You couldn't walk ten steps in Harlem without hearing about Lamar Williams and the legend of his "Sweet Feet."

Mike and I were once great players at the Park. But you're not a legend like "Sweet Feet" until you beat the best. This was our journey. And it all began six years earlier, right here, through the holes in the Park fence...

CHAPTER TWO

SHORTY

It was a perfect spring day for a sixth grader, not a cloud in the sky and just warm enough to wear shorts. This meant the Park would be packed. I guessed the Jungle courts were crowded that day. Some of the guys who usually played up there, walked six blocks south to beat up on us kids. There was a definite pecking order in Harlem hoops, and when you were a skinny twelve-year-old like me, you were right at the end of the line.

I easily passed through a hole in the fence and made my way onto the blacktop at the Park. Mike and I would play together on the Jungle courts someday, but not until I proved myself here. The brand of basketball at the Park was typical Harlem hoops. Always tough, always fast paced, and always filled with trash talk. I tried not to talk too much. After all, Mike did enough jawing for the both of us.

While I was stretching, a figure approached. He was

tall and wore his hair in dreadlocks. "What's up, Hope." He spoke confidently.

"What's up?" I replied, not sure who he was. "Do I know you?"

"Oh, *my bad*. You're not Mike Hope. You look like this kid I know." Mike had just hit a growth spurt and was now a full four inches taller than me. Somehow, people still had a hard time telling us apart.

A smaller friend of "dreadlocks" reached up to tap him on the shoulder, "That's Shorty, Mike Hope's little brother." I hated that nickname and I hated being thought of as Mike's younger brother.

"Actually I'm Tony, Mike's my twin." A lot of guys knew Mike. He was recognized as one of the top young players in Harlem. I guess these guys had seen him play.

The taller guy shook my hand. "I'm Jason, Jason Helms. You better know that name, Shorty." He rose his eyebrows in a cocky way. I *did* know that name. Jason used to play and dominate, here at the Park. He'd been playing up at the Jungle for the past two years, so we never got a chance to face off. "Tell your brother we need a fifth guy today."

After he realized I wasn't Mike, he lost interest in speaking with me and made his way toward his friends. I didn't want to waste this opportunity. "Uh…Mike's coming down later, but I can play until he gets here."

"No way, Shorty." He turned around with an annoyed look on his face. "When your brother comes down you let me know. I'm not trying to run training sessions for kids." He drew laughter from his friends. "We can't have some little midget running around on this court." They laughed again. Jason dribbled in the opposite direction.

The laughter grew until it echoed throughout the court. My heart pounded like a war drum. I'd reached my breaking point. An instant later I was running full speed toward the most feared player on the court. I came up behind him and knocked the ball out of his hands, making an easy lay up.

I pointed at Jason. "This little midget just made you look like a punk – punk!"

Jason grabbed me by the shirt. The next thing I remember was his arm extending back and his fist smacking against my jaw. I fell to the floor with a thump.

He stood over me. "You better learn to respect your elders, punk!" He grabbed the ball back and walked away.

I wiped some blood from my lower lip and yelled, "Hey, Jason!"

He turned and faced me, "What? You want some more of that Shorty?" The answer was no. I definitely didn't want any more of that, but a fire was burning inside me.

"You and me, one on one." I spoke before I fully thought about this proposition. Playing one on one against a player five inches taller, and four years older than me probably wasn't a good idea.

"What'd you just ask me?" Jason and his friends started laughing. Once again, I was the butt of their jokes. He casually sat down on a bench and sipped from his water bottle. "Go home, Shorty." He wasn't taking me seriously. No one was.

"Stand up and play me one on one to eleven, Jason." I spit blood onto the ground. "Or are you just a punk?" Everyone who was at the Park that day moved in a little bit closer. I heard some mumbling from the crowd. I was sure that what I'd just said was either going to get me hit in the face again or a one on one game with the best ballplayer on the court.

Kids I knew and people passing by were now perched on a bench, or leaning against the fence, watching it all unfold. The court began to clear as Jason took off his shirt and revealed an upper body that was twice the size of my own. I took my shirt off in response. It was not a pretty sight. My ribs stuck out, my arms were puny, and I don't think I could have intimidated a beanstalk. I stood there shirtless anyway.

Jason walked toward me and threw the ball hard at my chest. "Check it up, punk!"

I caught the ball. "One thing first. If I win, you get me an invite to the Jungle." Jason smiled, "Shorty, if you win I'll take you to the Amazon Jungle."

I bent down and tightened my shoelaces, cradling the ball under my left arm. Mom always told us to be confident and never feel intimidated. So when I rose up with my face three inches from Jason's chest, there was no fear in my eyes. "I'm not scared of you." I checked the ball.

Just as the game was about to start, Mike showed up. He stepped through one of the holes in the fence and slapped hands with a few of the neighborhood kids. As he made his way onto the court Jason had some words for him, "Your brother's got a bigger mouth than you, Mike. I'm about to shut it for him."

Mike ignored him and came directly over to me. He grabbed the ball from my hands sharply. "How'd this happen?"

He pointed to my swollen lip.

"I asked for it." I didn't want Mike involved.

He yelled over at Jason anyway. "You like picking on guys half your size?"

Jason laughed. "Shorty needs another couple of inches before he's half my size."

"Then why don't you play me, tough guy?" Mike began walking toward Jason.

I stepped in his path. "Let me handle this, Mike."

"You can handle this guy?" Mike looked over at Jason, then back at me.

I tried to grab the ball from him, but he wouldn't give it up. "Just let me play him. This is my problem."

Reluctantly, Mike dropped the ball back into my hands. "Well, now you've got another problem. This guy's a baller, T." This was a term used to describe a really talented basketball player. "You can beat him though. Don't back down. This is what we've been practicing for." He gave me a knuckle bump, staring at Jason as he walked toward the sideline. While many kids leaned against the fences, a seat on the bench was saved just for Mike. He was becoming a legend on these courts.

Jason stood in front of me in a weak defensive stance. He wasn't taking me and my twelve-year-old body seriously. On the first play I blew past him left, making an easy lay up. Jason obviously wasn't too rattled, because on my next possession his long arm swatted my shot routinely. He regained control of the loose ball and stood at the top of the key, talking trash, "Here it comes, Hope. Get ready."

I crouched down, getting set defensively. I would have

the most impact stopping the dribble, rather than trying to block shots. Many defenders like to watch the path of the ball, others like to look into their opponent's eyes. I stared at the hips. I learned that an offensive player wasn't going anywhere unless his hips shifted first. If Jason decided to move, I would know exactly where he was going before his feet did.

As Helms began to yo-yo the ball up and down with his right hand, he noticed my unorthodox defensive style and thought he had the perfect opportunity to open his mouth again. "Any of you guys have a spatula? I think Shorty's stuck to the - " Just as he was about to complete his insult, I sprouted out of my stance, knocking the ball away. I made another uncontested lay up, showboating this time with a pretty finger roll.

All of Jason's friends started jeering at him as I dribbled back to the top of the key. He'd been embarrassed on the court he used to own. Suddenly he looked like a middle linebacker about to drill a running back. His nostrils were flaring and beads of sweat dripped down his face. He charged, and began hand checking me with the force of a grizzly bear. I turned my back to him and was pelted by slaps on my wrists and forearms. A voice rang out from the crowd, "Hey, he's foulin' the kid! Play like a man, Helms!"

Despite the harassment, Jason wouldn't let up. He was smacking and pushing with all his force. I could only get knocked around for so long before I lost control of the ball. I had to do something.

After a few more bumps, I tried a play that I'd prac-ticed numerous times against my brother. I noticed Jason's legs were spread wide while he smacked and hacked at the backs of my arms. Normally I didn't set out to embarrass someone on the basketball court, but this was different. Not only had Jason disrespected my ability, he'd punched me in the mouth as well. I turned around and bounced the ball directly between his open legs. Then I darted past as he lunged for the rock. "Too late!" I exclaimed, grabbing the ball after two bounces and rolling in another lay up.

Jason's crew began to razz him even more, "Shorty's making you look stupid, Jay."

"Three-nothing, Hope!" Mike shouted from the sideline, a huge smile plastered to his face. Usually he was the victim of my between the legs fake out move.

A few of Jason's friends started cheering for me as well. "You're the man, Shorty! Show him what's up!" I started to sense that despite their friendships with my opponent, his crew couldn't help but pull for the upset.

Jason wisely changed his game plan after my early advantage. I was giving away five inches and at least fifty pounds to the sixteen-year-old giant, so utilizing his intimidating size rather than his mediocre ball handling skills was an obvious choice. He started backing the ball into the post, a tactic which offered me less of a chance to swipe the pill from him and a greater chance at a black eye. Bumping me backward about two or three feet gave him easy looks at short post shots. He began to score at will. Still, I continued jumping, swiping, shooting, sweating, and bleeding my way back into the game.

The score went back and forth for the next ten minutes. This was turning into a battle: my quickness against his size, his experience versus my youth, and his pride versus my will.

We were tied at ten in a game to eleven. Jason held the ball at the top of the key. Through heavy breaths he muttered, "Next hoop wins." I tried to keep my defensive intensity high, but my tired legs wouldn't cooperate. Jason turned his back to the basket and powered me deep into the post. I leaned my forearm into the middle of his back, desperately trying to hold my ground. I couldn't afford to let him move in any closer. But my last gasp was useless. Jason had progressed to the basket with relative ease. By the time he turned to face up, all that was left was a three-foot bank shot that he'd probably made a million times in his life. Make that a million and one.

He pumped his fist in the air victoriously and pulled on his shorts in exhaustion. I knew that when this game started he would never have imagined getting that fired up after beating a twelve-year-old kid by a single point. I put my hands on my hips, wondering if I should have tried for the steal on the last play of the game. Wondering when I would get another chance at an invite to the Jungle.

Jason came over to me and shook my hand with a smile on his face. "Nice game, Tony." I couldn't believe it! He called me Tony.

After that game I was always Tony. I had graduated; no one ever called me Shorty again. I had earned Jason's respect. I could see it in his face when he approached me, and felt it in the firmness of his handshake. He spoke to me before exiting through a hole in the fence. "You've got a ton of game, Tony. If you ever need someone to run with, come up to the Jungle. I'll play with you anytime."

I nodded my head, exhausted and beaten, but respected.

CHAPTER THREE

LOCKED OUT

It was close to nine o'clock. Memories of my childhood faded as Mike, Devon, and Nick continued past the Park. When they reached an empty parking lot they stopped and pulled their backpacks off, looking around cautiously. I followed from about twenty yards away, covered from view by a crooked fence that wrapped around the lot. A yellow light above the rusted sign, PARKING, shone softly on my brother and his friends. I stood in the shadows, seeing and hearing them clearly through the old, splintered wood.

Mike spoke, "Guys, I'm not too sure about going to this party." He sounded concerned.

Devon responded, "What's the matter, college boy, you scared of having some fun?"

Nick's obnoxious hyena laugh echoed into the night. He slapped five with Devon.

"Yeah college boy, still got time to run home to Mama." His

stupid laugh continued.

Mike forced a smile. This image of indifference didn't fool me. He was nervous. I had to find out why.

One by one the guys unzipped their packs. I leaned in closer to the fence, trying to get a clear view. Devon reached deep into his backpack and pulled out a paper bag. The three of them gathered in close. I squinted to get a peek, but my line of sight was blocked by their tight circle. My concentration was broken by the sounds of an approaching car. "Get down!" Devon pointed to his left, diving behind a nearby dumpster in a panic. Mike and Nick followed like they were playing a game of Simon Says.

An instant later a New York City police car rolled up to the empty lot. The street became library quiet. A flashlight shined on the front of the oversized trash bin and the officer peered out of her window suspiciously. Mike crouched as low as he could, holding on to the side of the filthy dumpster for balance. His arms were shaking and his legs were buried in the overflow of garbage. I turned and sat motionless with my back to the action. I couldn't bear to look anymore. Soon the flash of light disappeared and all that was left were sighs and laughter. The police car was gone.

My brother, less than a day away from a college scholarship, was ducking behind trash to avoid the law. What was he doing? He knew we had to get to the NBA, show Mom a better life. I pictured her, sweating in our tiny apartment with no fans or air conditioning, fighting with rats and cockroaches, sipping tap water from a leaky faucet. Had Mike forgotten Mom?

The guys scraped trash from their clothes and arrived at the corner of 151st Street and 1st Avenue completely out of breath. They'd reached a crossroad. I automatically assumed they would be going west, toward civilization. I was wrong. They went east, toward the river. There were only two things east of 1st Avenue and 151st Street: our old high school and trouble. Since I knew that Mike wasn't going back to catch up on his studies at ten o'clock at night in the middle of August, I was sure he was looking for trouble. He was going to a place in Harlem where drugs and violence ran the streets.

The stakes had been raised. I followed closer. A few minutes later, I stopped at the front steps of our high school. Mike was fifty feet ahead as he passed by the back door to our old gymnasium.

The concrete steps leading to the main entrance seemed more cracked than they were just a few months ago. Every window was barricaded with metal bars and stained with rust. The painted front door was two shades of ugly brown and the sign reading 'Public School 44' was hanging upside down, the handiwork of some hooligan. When principals and security guards went home for the summer, this was what PS-44 became.

I imagined my new life at UNY, fourteen hours and counting. Tomorrow the stairs would be perfect, the windows clean. Students would line the streets and fresh coats of royal blue and orange paint would adorn brand new signs for the University of New York.

I moved forward quietly, the darkness disguising me. I could still hear my brother's voice up the street. Fifty feet later

I was standing alone in front of our old gym. I tugged on a chain that barricaded the entrance. I remembered the first time I was locked out of that gym...

After my game against Jason Helms everything changed. Mike and I started playing at the Jungle and the buzz about us in the neighborhood grew. People all over New York City were talking about the Hope brothers. In fact, the New York Times ran an article about two fourteen-year-old twins from Harlem who had a shot at the NBA. While Mike took these comments in stride, I let the praise go straight to my head. Mike was used to people telling him that he was great. I wasn't. So by the time I entered the gym for the first day of high school tryouts, my arrogant attitude had me believing that I deserved special treatment.

"On your wing, T. Ball, ball, ball," Mike was running alongside me on the fast break with one man guarding the basket. Instead of throwing a routine bounce pass, I forced my shoulder into the chest of the scrawny defender at the top of the key. Once I had him reeling backward, I picked up my dribble and tossed Mike what I thought was a perfect alley-oop pass. Normally, he would catch the feed and bash home a monstrous dunk. Only this time, the ball rose above his outstretched arms and ricocheted off the backboard. I'd blown an easy fast break.

The bruised defender picked up the ball and sprinted down the court untouched. Coach Walter Harris glared at me. I returned the stare.

While Mike hustled full speed down the court in an effort to prevent an easy basket, I casually jogged down the floor. I knew I'd made a mistake, but I also knew that I had a spot on the varsity team - no matter what happened during these tryouts.

After our opponents scored another easy lay up, I took the in bounds pass and dribbled up the floor with a kick to my step. We were down by one point in a game to eleven. I knew we needed a score. This was my chance to impress Coach. I dribbled the ball over the half court stripe, ignoring an open man on my right.

The defender guarding me was a step slow. I could have breezed by him at any time. Sure, a lay up would have tied the game, but I wanted to show off my jump shot. Coach needed to see *all* my skills. I dribbled around the swinging arms of the frenzied defender until my body was parallel to Coach's, four feet beyond the arc. I shot a glance toward the sideline. "Watch this Coach." He rolled his eyes.

With a convincing head fake forward I was able to gain a step between myself and my opponent. Mike saw the desire in my eyes, and as usual, he was there to assist me. He set a brutal pick, which meant that Mike used his body to block my defender. This left me with an open look at a long jump shot. I squared my body toward the basket and made certain my form was flawless, elbow tucked, knees bent, high extension and release. I was sure this shot would be the perfect redemption for my previous miscues.

I held my exaggerated follow through. "That's money," I said, waiting for the ball to swish through the net. My confident smile soured as I watched the ball run out of gas on the way to the rim. The shot dropped two feet short of the hoop, an embarrassing air ball. I shook my head in disbelief and trudged down the court to play defense.

"Hey Hope! Do you always hold your follow through on air balls?" Coach Harris was furious. "Stop the game for a second." Squeaking sneakers and the rhythmic thumping of the bouncing ball ceased. All that was left was the thunder of Coach's voice in the old gymnasium. "All I see is playground in you, Hope. The alley-oops, the fast breaks, the lack of hustle and the crazy shots from half court. Play the game the way it was meant to be played, with your teammates, not against them!" This was not what I expected on the first day of try-outs. "It's not just you and Michael out there, look to pass to someone else." He blew his whistle, "Get some water guys."

I couldn't believe that Coach had cut the game short. Everyone gathered by the bleachers, drinking water and sharing strange looks. But I stayed on the court with Coach. The game wasn't over yet. Mike looked at me as if he could see smoke blowing from my ears. He motioned with his hands, pushing his palms toward the floor, a signal to calm me down. He knew I was about to explode. I could hear Mike's voice, "Stay cool, T."

I ignored this voice. A heated dialogue was circling inside my head. I'm a great player. Last week Mike and I had our pictures in the New York Times! Coach Harris never had his picture in the Times. What was he doing by embarrassing me in front of my new teammates? Who did this man think he was? I continued my inner monologue, I'm fourteen-years-old and half the Division I college basketball programs in the country are already drooling over me. The only person I know who can still hang with me is Mike, and when we're on the same team, that game's over before it starts. Coach Harris knows this! So why is he disrespecting me?

I stood deep in thought at center court. Coach stared at me, waiting for my next move. "Are you gonna join your teammates or do you have something you'd like to say?"

I became even more enraged. "This is the first time you've ever seen me play, Coach. How can you tell that I'm all playground?" I raised my voice, "And besides, whether I'm playground or not, I have skills. If you were a real coach, you'd understand that much."

Coach Harris moved closer to me. My fourteen-year-old frame stood tall to face him. I wouldn't back down an inch. "Are you telling me how to do my job, Hope?" He moved to my right side, his face about three inches from my ear. "I've been coaching kids like you for thirty years. You know how long that is?"

I spoke loudly, "If you can't handle us anymore, maybe you should retire."

His voice crashed down like a bolt of lightning, "When you're in this gym, you are in *my* house!" I flinched backward. Coach, a mountain of a man, at six-feet-four inches tall and at least two hundred and fifty pounds, was screaming, "And nobody, *nobody*, is gonna disrespect me in my house! Do you understand me?" His chest was heaving.

I didn't answer.

"I said do you understand me?"

I deliberately paused. "Yeah, whatever," I said nonchalantly.

Mike walked onto the court, "Coach, can I say something?"

Coach answered promptly, "Go back with your teammates, Michael. You're brother owes me an apology." He stared at me again. "Well?"

I remember thinking that I had to establish myself early in this relationship. Coach needed me for the next four years and he was going to respect my game whether he liked it or not. There would be no apology. I looked up at him in a defining moment. "Coach, I think the only person who needs to be apologizing is you, for disrespecting me in front of my teammates."

Coach shrugged his shoulders. "Okay. If that's how you want to do it, you're out of here. I'm the guy blowing the whistle, not you." He pointed an enormous finger at me, "You have no respect for your elders, and until you learn that, you're not welcome anywhere near this gym. So collect your stuff and get out of here."

I stepped back in disbelief. Had I just gotten thrown off the team? My hands shook as I grabbed my book bag from a hook on the back wall. I approached the exit to the gym and turned around before leaving. "You've got no idea who you're sending home." Everyone was dead silent, staring. I couldn't look at my brother. I didn't want to see the disappointment on his face. I put my backpack on my shoulder and left. When I closed the door to the gym that day, it locked behind me.

CHAPTER FOUR

SWEET FEET

I continued past my old gym, following the guys east down 151ˢᵗ Street. One block away was the building Lamar "Sweet Feet" Williams grew up in. When I was in grade school we used to come down to his apartment every day after class. There would usually be about three or four of us, and we'd stand on each other's shoulders to get a closer look into his second story window. After everyone had gone home, Mike and I would talk about "Sweet Feet." We were probably his biggest fans. Though Lamar has long since moved out, his apartment is a constant reminder of his place in Harlem's history.

When the guys approached the building, Nick pointed toward Lamar's window. I waited for Mike to go through his routine. Normally he'd stand on the tips of his toes to catch a glimpse into the legend's apartment. He'd move his head from side to side, getting different viewpoints, dreaming of what might be. We desperately wanted to be known as Harlem's greatest basketball players, the title currently owned by "Sweet Feet."

But on this night, Mike didn't look up. In fact, he did everything in his power to avoid Lamar's place. He passed by, kicking a Coke can back and forth with Nick, missing the coolest sight in all of Harlem. In that window hangs a pair of size twelve basketball sneakers. The same pair "Sweet Feet" wore for every game he played at Public School 44. They hung as a tribute, they added to his legend. The shoelaces dangled, the tongue was ripped, the sole was worn and the color had faded from white to gray. Every time I saw those old shoes I felt a tap on the shoulder, a kick in the pants, sometimes I'd even hear them whisper, "You can do it, Tony."

I crept closer to the guys, afraid to lose them around the next dark corner. Flickering streetlights and patches of fog made my pursuit doubly difficult. My tired eyes squinted through the haze to get a better look at the sneakers.

"Hey Tony!" A voice rang out from the darkness.

I jumped back, startled, as Mike approached me, "What are you doing here?" He asked.

I guess I wasn't cut out to be a spy after all. I'd been busted, "I...um..."

A split second later the guys joined Mike in a semicircle around me. "What is this, a family reunion?" Devon's sarcastic comment made my stomach turn.

Mike moved closer to me, "Tony, what are you doing? I thought you didn't want to come with us."

I snapped, "I don't know where you idiots are taking

Mike, or what you're doing, but I've got a bad feeling about this party. Lloyd said that - "

Nick burst out laughing, "Lloyd Bright! That guy's more uptight than you, Tony."

I ignored Nick. "Let's go home, Mike. We start college tomorrow, remember? We still have to pack up all our stuff and -"

Now Devon butted in, "Listen T, he'll pack up tomorrow morning." He looked over at Mike, "You can pack in the morning, can't you?"

Mike answered, unsure, "Yeah, of course I can. I can pack tomorrow, real early, T."

I stared at my brother, "Make your own decision, Mike. We've worked too hard for you to get into trouble the night before - "

Devon started laughing, cutting me off again, "What trouble? It's a party! You ever leave the Jungle long enough to go to a party?"

Mike put his hand on Devon's chest, "Shut up, Devon."

Devon glanced my way, "We're just gonna celebrate a little tonight. You should loosen up and join us, Tony."

I shot a look at my brother, "I'm asking you to come home with me."

Nick put his arm on Mike's shoulder, "Let's go, Mike, be your own man."

Nick and Devon turned and started walking down 151st. I stood on the sidewalk, staring at my twin brother as he backpedaled away from me, "Don't be so dramatic, T. Everything's cool. Go home and get some sleep, I'll be all right." I watched Mike get smaller and smaller, fading into the darkness. A feeling of helplessness overcame me, there was nothing more I could do. The time for spying was over. I gave up and started the walk home.

I remembered the last time I was spying. Back then, I wasn't looking for Mike. I was looking for my spot on the varsity basketball team...

Two and a half months after being kicked out of Coach Harris's gym, I started to really miss the game. I'd been working over at Soapy Sid's Car Wash every day after school. The only way I kept my game sharp was by firing soggy towels into nearby buckets. If towel basketball ever became a sport, I'd be a pro for sure. I even beat the owner, Soapy Sid himself, in a game to fifteen. And that guy had been shooting towels for thirty years! Aside from a little fun, working at the car wash was hard. When I came home at night, my blistered hands would barely be able to hold a basketball. But they *were* able to sneak twenty dollar bills into Mom's purse after she fell asleep. This was the one thing that made me smile in my new life without hoops.

One Tuesday afternoon I came home a little early from work. When I walked through the door, Mom's heavy breathing filled the dark living room. She was sound asleep on the couch, her aged cloth bag on the floor next to her. She started work at 3:45 every morning, so by the afternoon, she needed a nap. I didn't want to turn the light on and wake her up. I crept through the darkness, to Mom's side. I reached into my pocket and pulled out a wad of cash. Then, I stealthily unzipped Mom's bag, dropping in that day's pay. "Tony, what are you doing in my purse?" I jumped back. Mom had been awake the whole time. "I've been noticing extra money in my wallet recently. In the fifteen years that you've been alive, have you ever seen me with extra money?" She sat upright, her expression turned serious. "I know what you've been doing. You're a good boy, Tony."

I sat down next to my mother, who rubbed my back lovingly.

She reached into her bag and handed me a wad of cash, every dollar I had given her for the past two months. She hadn't spent a penny. "This is your money. You earned it, Tony. After your father left us..." She paused. Mom never talked about him. "I knew life would be tough on you boys. But I never asked for your help paying the bills. That's my job. Your job's to go after your dreams, get your education, and look out for your brother. I'll keep looking out for this family — same way I've been doing since I carried you two in my belly."

"I just wanted to help you." I rested my head on Mom's shoulder.

She kissed my forehead. "You need to go back to playing basketball. That's what makes you happy. I like life the way it's always been, an empty wallet and smiles." She stood up. "Now I've *really* got to get some sleep." She laughed as she made her way into her bedroom. "Always could fake you out."

Mom was right. The team needed me and I needed basketball. Varsity practice was about to start, and I was going. These would be my first steps onto a basketball court since my run in with Coach Harris. I hurriedly threw on a pair of shorts and laced up my sneakers.

The team was only a few days away from its first round playoff game against Hamilton High. The guys had a decent regular season, winning fourteen and losing ten. Still, they hadn't lived up to preseason expectations. A New York Times article had claimed that the Hope Brothers were "a tandem that would take high school basketball at Public School 44 to the next level." With me on the couch, the chances of hanging a state championship banner had vanished. The guys needed me out there.

When I arrived at school, the afternoon silence was broken by the gentle sweeping of a night custodian's broom. I moved toward the gym, my footsteps resonating loudly through the hallway. The pounding of my feet against the floor was interrupted by the faint bouncing of basketballs.

"Come on guys, keep hustling!" Coach Harris' voice and the blowing of his whistle jolted me. I peeked around the corner at the entrance to the gym, which was cracked open. The foot stand was pressed against the floor, opening a three inch window. I came to the heavy door and grabbed the handle, trying to spy through the crack without being noticed. Mike congratulated teammates after scoring the winning hoop in a scrimmage game. Five other guys trudged over to the water fountain. You could always tell which team lost in practice because they were the first to get a drink.

My ear pressed closer to the action. I started to remember the way people sounded on a basketball court. "Well done, Michael." Coach Harris was pleased. "You guys are really starting to come together."

I wanted a piece of that game, but my pride kept me from mustering up the courage to enter. Through the slit in the door, I watched half of practice. They *were* coming together. In between jumpers and rebounds, Mike laughed with his friends and joked around. Teammates slapped five and bumped knuckles. Mom was right. I did miss basketball, only basketball didn't seem to miss me. A strange notion occurred in those moments; maybe PS-44 didn't need Tony Hope after all. This thought was overwhelming. I could only bear to watch practice for a few more minutes. Then I left, broken.

I came home later that night and found my brother wrestling with our old television set, trying to get a clear picture for the start of SportsCenter. Our schedules had been conflicting and I felt like I hadn't seen Mike in weeks. We slapped hands. "Nice seeing you, T. How's Soapy Sid's going?" Mike smiled at me as I took a bite of his ham sandwich that sat on the coffee table.

I spoke with my mouth full. "It's all right. Beat Sid in towel hoops." I swallowed. "How's the team?"

"Decent. But we've got no point guard. I'm trying to win a state championship and you're playing towel hoops."

I changed the subject. "TV broken again?"

"This thing's always busted." Mike grabbed his sandwich away from me.

The television reception began to improve and he moved away from the set. I leaned forward. "So there's something I want to talk to you about. I know you're waiting for me to apologize to Coach Harris. But I'll be honest with you, it's not gonna happen."

Mike spoke with half a sandwich stuffed in his cheeks. "What do you mean it's not gonna to happen? You know how bad I need you out there? Nobody knows where I'm going on the break. Dizzy's playing the point now, and all he's doing is making *me* dizzy."

I sat down next to Mike and chuckled. "Dizzy's running the point?" Dizzy was a player I had schooled for years at the playground courts. There was a guy like Dizzy on every high school basketball team. He was the nicest guy in the world, but he wasn't a ballplayer.

Mike swallowed loudly. "You've got to apologize to Coach Harris. If you don't, you can forget about playing next year." He sat up sharply and clicked the television off.

I couldn't look at him. "What if I don't want to play next year?"

"You don't want to play?" Mike sounded shocked, "Tony, we were supposed to be the two best players in Harlem. One argument with a coach and you're finished? Don't you still love this game?"

"Coach Harris disrespected me."

"Who cares, Tony? I asked you a question, do you still love basketball?"

I stared at the floor. "Of course I still love basketball."

Mike stood up. "Good. I have something for you then. If you said you didn't love basketball, I was gonna have to take Dizzy."

I followed him curiously. "Take Dizzy where? What do you got?" Mike didn't answer, tip-toeing through the hallway past Mom's room. I whispered, "Hey, where you going?"

He still wouldn't answer. When we stepped into our bedroom he opened the top drawer of his dresser, reaching under his smelly socks. "You're really not going to apologize to Coach? You know, I shouldn't even be giving you this." He handed me a pair of tickets.

My eyes widened when I saw the logo of the New York Pride. Somehow, Mike had gotten us seats for Lamar Williams's final game at Towers Memorial Arena. The game had been sold out for months. I stared at him in disbelief, hiding my smile. "How'd you get these?"

He dropped the tickets on the dresser, "So, are you through with basketball or do you want to go see "Sweet Feet?"

The nickname "Sweet Feet" was one Lamar earned on the streets of Harlem. Back when he was thirteen-years-old people would come from all over New York City just to watch him dribble the basketball. During his four years at PS-44, the legend of Lamar Williams grew until every kid in New York had heard of his "Sweet Feet." His size twelves put our high school on the map.

Tilting and twisting our old antenna to the perfect angle was the only way I got to catch a glimpse of my favorite player. Sometimes I would have to wrap tin foil around the crooked metal thing in order to see my hero cross over an opponent or hit a game winning shot. I'd watch him through the fuzzy reception and imitate every move he made from our living room floor. So how could I pass up a trip to watch him play in person?

Two weeks later, Mike and I were six rows deep in the stands at Towers Memorial. I sat upright, watching the greatest basketball player in the world in his final game. Once the ball had tipped, I stopped thinking about my troubles and just watched "Sweet Feet." He stood six-feet-two inches tall, with short black hair and light brown skin. The wrinkles on his face were the product of an enormous smile that seemed to grow from his ears.

Lamar played inspired that night. Even at thirty-seven years of age, his feet danced like he was starring in a Broadway musical. His aging knees and bad back had forced him to retire, but the way he moved that night, you would have thought he could play forever.

With the Pride up by fifteen late in the fourth quarter, Lamar dribbled the ball patiently at the top of the key. He waved his hands, directing traffic. A young defender began shuffling his feet, knowing that something was coming. Lamar faked to his left, smiling at the kid who couldn't have been a day over twenty-one. This guy had no chance.

Then "Sweet Feet" rocketed right with the youngster trailing a step behind like a puppy following his master. An open lane cleared and Lamar dribbled toward the basket. A giant center quickly clogged the middle, forcing a shot. Lamar jumped. The seven-footer leaped into the air as well, his mouth watering for a piece of the basketball.

In an acrobatic airborne move, Lamar brought the ball back down to his waist and whipped a pass around the back of the giant defender. The ball landed softly in the hands of a cutting Chris Tomey, who jammed home the leather. Lamar had worked his magic one last time.

After the game, Mike and I waited outside the Pride

locker room for "Sweet Feet." There were probably close to fifty other people lining the tunnel that led to the parking lot. Forty-five minutes of staring at closed doors felt more like two hours. Finally, security guards emerged, clearing a path for the players. First came Tom Jones, a seven-foot center who looked like a flagpole, then Mark Tinzon rumbled out, the power forward who must have been born in a weight room. Then, out of the darkness, came a familiar smile. Lamar Williams stood three feet away from us, dressed in a light brown suit, and toting a gym bag on his right shoulder.

He stood tall above the crowd, wading through people with the same unaffected smoothness he displayed on the basketball court. Kids tugged at his side, pleading for autographs. One went as far as wrapping himself around Lamar's enormous leg. "Sweet Feet" laughed calmly, the youngster still attached. "Hey guys, give me a little space and I'll get to all of you. Let's try and make a line. I'll sign for everyone."

People bullied for position frantically as Mike and I watched the line form in front of us. When the dust settled, we were dead last. Lamar sat in a chair with a small table in front of him, signing autographs for wide-eyed kids who'd waited their entire lives for this moment.

Twenty minutes and a pretzel later, our moment had arrived. "We're going to miss you, Mr. Williams." I shook his hand firmly as I spoke.

Mike shook next. "My brother and I grew up watching you play. It's gonna be tough watching the Pride without you."

"Thanks guys." Lamar grabbed two five-by-eight photos of himself from a box on the corner of the table. "Who should I sign these to?"

Mike introduced us, "I'm Mike Hope and this is my brother Tony."

Lamar's eyes lit up. "You're not the Hope brothers from Harlem, are you?"

I was shocked that Lamar Williams knew who we were. "How'd you know that?"

"I read that article about you two in the Times, said you guys could play some ball. So, how'd the season go?"

Mike spoke because I couldn't, "The season went okay. We lost a tough one to Carver in the state quarterfinals. We should be able to get them next year — if we can get this guy back on the team." Mike patted me on the shoulder and smiled. I tried to smile along with him.

"Sweet Feet's" head shifted in my direction. "What do you mean, *back* on the team?" His gaze was intense, smile broken. "Why were you off the team in the first place?"

I hung my head as I spoke, "I had an argument with Coach Harris and decided that I didn't want to play for him."

"What do you mean *you* decided? That's not your choice." Lamar spoke sternly, "That article said you guys loved playing this game and that you were dreaming of the NBA. That's a tough road, boys. Look around you, every NBA player that passes through these doors has had a coach that he didn't want to play for. Did they quit? Did they disrespect him? No."

I wanted to say something. "Mr. Williams, the NBA is a dream of mine but — "

"But nothing!" Lamar stopped me short, pointing his finger. "You go back and apologize to Coach Harris. You think I always got along with him when he was my Coach?" He placed his hand on my shoulder and asked me a question that would change my life: "Every dream has a price. Are you willing to pay? Think about it."

CHAPTER FIVE

SKIPPIN' OUT

It was a clear night by New York City standards. I even managed to catch a glimpse of some stars in between tall buildings. A full moon shone brightly. My senses were heightened. I heard a car screech a few blocks away. Someone was blaring their radio in the distance. Two men fought over a half-eaten cheeseburger. A young woman on a cell phone argued with a friend as she sped past. The Harlem streets were wide-awake. My brother could stay out all night if he wanted to, but I was going home. Tomorrow was a big day.

About ten minutes into my walk, I saw a familiar face sitting on a nearby bench. Cheryl Phelps, a friend from high school, smiled and waved. She was a year younger than me, and planned on attending UNY when she graduated. "Tony, what are you doing here?" She motioned with her hand. "Sit down."

She was a tiny girl with dark brown skin and curly hair

that she wore in a ponytail. I sat down next to her. Cheryl
threw a couple of crumbs from a bag of bread she'd brought to
feed the pigeons. "Why are you so quiet?" She asked.

I grabbed a piece of bread, tossing a few crumbs. "No
reason. I'm leaving tomorrow and everything."

Cheryl nodded her head. "Where's Mike?"

"He went to that party."

She paused, nervously. "With who?" Cheryl always
asked a lot of questions.

"Nick and Devon, why?" I asked.

Her expression changed. "I heard Trevor Samuels was
out to get Nick and Devon. It could get ugly tonight. You should
get your brother out of there. You know Mike, he doesn't see
the bad in those guys."

My heart started racing. "Where's the party, Cheryl?

"Over on 153rd Street. In that old warehouse on the
corner."

"I gotta go." I jumped up from the bench and started
running...

"Run Hope, run!" Coach Harris was always screaming
at me. Our last practice of my sophomore season was no different. " I didn't let you back on this team so you could jog
down the floor!" I ran back on defense as hard as I could, still
he constantly reminded me of my freshman mistake.

My ten assists per game during my first high school
season proved to Coach that I was more than just a selfish
playground player. But our sophomore year didn't end with
playoff glory. We lost in the opening round to Douglass High
by fifteen points. The only good news was that my breakout

season had me looking toward a bright basketball future. Mike and I had our sights set on attending The University of New York, just like "Sweet Feet."

I spent the summer before my junior year washing cars at Soapy Sid's. This time, I had a partner. Mike and I would work the morning shift together, and dry off our hands for afternoons at the Jungle. Mom even agreed to let us give her a couple of dollars a week, so she could buy herself a present. She ended up replacing her tired purse with a brand new leather one.

That summer came and went the way summertime always does. Those twelve weeks felt more like twelve minutes. Before I realized what had happened, I was back in school for my junior year.

Although the team's sophomore campaign ended with a playoff loss, a year later something clicked. A strong junior season was backed by three straight post-season victories over top city schools. Brooklyn Central High was our final hurdle. If Mike and I outplayed "Brooklyn's Backcourt," James Thomas and Walter Randolph, we'd prove that we were the two best guards in the city. More importantly, we'd be state champions.

Two days prior to the state championship game, I walked into the cafeteria just before Mike and the guys showed up. My fourth period class was right next to the lunch room, so I was always the first one there. Usually, the guys jumped in line with me when they arrived. This wasn't technically cutting, because I saved them a spot, whatever that meant. But when I showed up at the cafeteria on this day, I was starving. I was already halfway through my lunch by the time the guys got there. If I ate fast enough, I would have a few minutes to shoot around in the gym before sixth period. After all, the biggest game of my life was just around the corner. When the team walked in, weaving in between the long tables the way they did defenders, I drew some serious stares. I hadn't saved anyone a spot in line.

Lunchtime in high school was always fun. For fifty minutes, science books and calculators were stuffed into filthy lockers. Talking without raising your hand was okay too, so the noise level was deafening.

Our cafeteria was shaped like a big square with long tables stretching across the room in several columns. We were in the back row, the basketball table. There weren't assigned seats, but everyone pretty much knew where to go. Mike sat to my left and Jermaine Smith was across from me. 'Smitty's' mom would make his lunch everyday. Watching him devour a tuna fish and pickle sandwich was just about the most disgusting thing in the world. Never mind the smell. Dizzy was to my right, and the rest of the team scattered on all sides of Mike.

I finished my gourmet lunch: a paper thin cheeseburger, a cardboard container of chocolate milk, and a rancid cup of fruit. Just as I was rising to my feet to toss my tray into the garbage, Mike pushed down on my shoulders. "Forget to say hello to your brother?" He sat down, biting into his cheeseburger. "These are great today."

Dizzy sat down on my right. "Did you understand what Mrs. Nelson was talking about in chemistry, T?" He took a bite of his burger and spit it back out. "I think mine went bad."

Mike grabbed the burger from Dizzy and ate the rest of it. "I think they're great."

Chemistry was one of my favorite subjects. I was always explaining stuff to Dizzy. "She was talking about neutrons and electrons. Those little particles that - " Dizzy had stopped listening and was staring at a table of girls across the way. I stopped talking and stared along with him.

Smitty unwrapped his tuna and pickle sandwich. I closed my eyes as he took his first bite. When I stood up to leave, Smitty spoke, mashing food in his mouth. "Wherg er yer gering?"

"What?" Dizzy, Mike and I, all asked at once.

Smitty swallowed. "Where are you going?"

Now the guys were looking at me. "I'm gonna shoot around for a few minutes in the gym."

Dizzy rolled his eyes. Smitty picked a piece of pickle off of the table and tossed it into his mouth. Mike patted my back. "If practice made perfect, you'd never miss a shot, T."

Just as I was about to walk away, Samantha Lewis, the prettiest girl in school, approached our table. Dizzy nodded his head, trying to look cool. "What's up?" His voice cracked and he did his best not to blush.

Samantha leaned over the table, talking directly to Mike, "Do you guys think you'd want to skip out on school for the rest of the day and go to the zoo?"

We all looked at one another with wide eyes. A tough proposition to refuse. Mike answered for all of us. "Absolutely."

Samantha smiled. "Great. Meet us out front in fifteen

minutes."

She left the table, and Rick Haynes, our power forward, spoke from a few seats down. "Where are we going?" He asked with a mischievous grin.

Mike was the captain of the team, the pilot. When he spoke, everyone followed his directions. As close as I was to him, even I had a tough time telling him no. Maybe it was the way he passed through life, like he had everything figured out. Still, he didn't understand that some risks weren't worth taking.

I took him aside for a minute. "This is stupid, Mike. We've got the state championship game in two days. If you get caught, they won't let you play."

He stood up, smiling at the table. "Well boys," I thought that maybe I had talked some sense into him, "let's not get caught." He winked at me. I had to laugh. As usual, Mike wasn't going to change his mind.

I spoke to the group, "If Coach finds out, you idiots are in serious trouble."

Paul Miller, our center, and the biggest guy in school agreed with me. "Yeah, I'm not going either. Can't risk it."

Mike smiled. "I think Samantha likes you, Paul. She was staring right at you."

Paul looked over at me. "Sorry T, I gotta go."

I shook my head. "I'm going to shoot around. Practice starts in four hours, make sure you guys get back in time."

Mike slapped me five. "Work on hitting those threes, we're gonna need to light up the board against Brooklyn Central." He left the cafeteria. Dizzy, Paul, Rick and Jermaine followed.

Practice started at three o'clock that afternoon. I was there at two, right after the last bell rang. During the hour, guys started trickling in. They changed, and came out to shoot around before Coach showed up. Mike still hadn't arrived at 2:57, and my eyes were everywhere looking for him. The door to the gym was wide open, giving me a clear view of the front door to the school. This was the only entrance to the school left unlocked after class ended. If Mike made it back from the zoo at all, this was his only way in.

The clock struck 3:01. Coach Harris was also late. My brother must have been the luckiest person in the world. This was the first time Coach had missed the start of practice during my two years on the team.

I shot three pointers from the left corner of the court. This was where I had the best view of the front door. It opened and closed numerous times, but Mike hadn't walked through. "Hello gentlemen." Coach Harris' voice rang out. He looked at the clock on the wall, 3:05. "Sorry I'm late." Everyone was at practice with the exception of Mike, Dizzy, Paul, Jermaine and Rick. We all looked around, hoping Coach wouldn't notice. But this was *his* team, he realized we were missing guys immediately. Coach approached me. "Where's your brother?"

I paused. I didn't know what to say. Then I watched the front door to the school open over Coach's left shoulder. Mike gave me a look and darted toward the back door to the locker room. The guys followed. Coach repeated himself, "Where is your brother? And where's Dizzy and Rick? Paul and Jermaine? What's going on here?"

I didn't want to lie to Coach. But the guys had arrived, and if I could just stall him for a second, everything would be all right. "Um, I think they're changing."

Coach threw me a curve. "I've got to go talk to them." He started walking toward the locker room. They would never make it to the court in time.

I jumped in front of Coach.

The rest of the team must have thought I had gone crazy. Coach looked puzzled. "Tony, what are you doing?"

I wasn't exactly sure, so I made something up. "When we run our zone defense am I supposed to drop down if they pass the ball into the post?" I hoped this question would buy Mike and the guys enough time to make their way onto the floor.

Coach walked to the free throw line and began explaining, "If their guard passes the ball into the post, you can drop down, but you've got to keep an eye on those guards outside." He stood in a defensive stance, showing me the correct position. "You lose track of those guards, they'll rain three pointers on us all day." He paused. "Okay?"

The truth was, I understood our defensive scheme perfectly. I nodded my head.

Coach walked back toward the locker room. I was panicked. Had Mike made it? Just as Coach was about to open the door, it opened in front of him. Mike, Dizzy, Jermaine, Paul and Rick stumbled out of the locker room, lacing up their sneakers and tucking in their practice jerseys.

Coach glared at them suspiciously. "Glad you could make it. Now let's get to work."

That practice was exhausting. We spent most of the two and a half hours running up and down the court like robots. When the whistle blew at five thirty, we took a knee around Coach. He delivered a short speech about the importance of teammates.

We went to the showers after he'd finished. "Tony." He called out to me just before I stepped into the locker room. "Can I please see you in my office?"

My heart raced. Coach knew that I wasn't confused about our zone defense, and that I was stalling for Mike and the guys. This was the same man who had kicked me off of his team two years ago. I was sure that, once again, I had fallen onto his bad side.

I sat down across from Coach in a wood chair that creaked for mercy. "Tony, I know what you did today." I put my hands over my head. He *did* know. "Your brother, Jermaine, Rick, Paul and Dizzy are not going to play in the state championship game. I knew they missed school before I got to practice today. That's why I was late. Principal Moscati informed me that they'll all be suspended, and won't be eligible for the game. I'm real disappointed with your brother." He paused. "But that's not what I want to talk to you about. What you did today, trying to distract me while the boys snuck around back, well, it was very brave. Your heart was in the right place. You looked out for your teammates and I don't know if you would have done that two years ago. You've really grown."

Coach was proud of me, but I was devastated. We'd worked so hard to get to the state championship game, now we would be playing short handed. With Mike out, I didn't know what to do. I'd never played without my wing-man.

We ended up getting humiliated against Brooklyn Central. We lost the game, the state championship, and the title of the best pair of guards in the city.

When the final buzzer sounded, we'd scored thirty-one fewer points than our opponent. James Thomas, who had outplayed me all night, had something to say, "Hey Hope, I thought you were gonna give us a game." Thomas mockingly waved at Mike, who sat on the bench in jeans. "You're not much without your brother."

After the game, Mike made me a promise: "I'll never leave you alone out there again."

CHAPTER SIX

FORTY-FOUR

I had to stop my brother before he got near that party.

I sprinted back toward Lamar's place where I'd left Mike and the guys. For the first time in my life, I ran past his window like it wasn't even there. I continued another block or so toward 153ʳᵈ. I didn't have much time. I'd left the guys about fifteen minutes ago. They had to be near the party by now.

I started running left and noticed hordes of people exiting the crowded warehouse. What was happening? I dashed across the street to get a closer look. My eyes were everywhere, searching for my brother. I stepped over the cracked sidewalk leading to the building — "Bang! Bang! Bang!" The loudest noise I'd ever heard rang out. Immediately, I fell to the floor, covering my head with my hands. "Bang! Bang!" I heard the noise again, this time followed by the sound of breaking glass.

Each time the noise exploded into the air my entire body

jolted. A few more teenagers running from the warehouse dropped to the floor around me. "Bang! Bang!" A woman held her two-year-old daughter close to her chest on the ground. "Somebody's shooting!" She screamed.

I stood up from the sidewalk, listening to sirens in the distance. "Mike! Hope!" I yelled into the night.

I bolted toward the front of the warehouse as people poured out onto the street. I searched for Mike's face in the mayhem...

I scanned through hundreds of faces in the crowd for one that looked like Mike's. We'd left the apartment together for a day at the Jungle, but somewhere in the chaos the two of us had separated. It was the fourth of July, and the Independence Day Parade was marching straight through Harlem. A band pounded their drums. Thousands of people lined the streets, waving American flags and cheering. With everyone wearing red, white and blue, it was like playing a real life game of 'Where's Waldo.'

When I couldn't find him, I figured he was already at the Jungle. Mike and I did everything but sleep down there during the summer before our senior season. We were on a mission to win the state championship.

In years past, we'd watch the parade from Dizzy's balcony, slurping on ice cream cones in the awful heat. But this summer, I didn't have time for ice cream. I waved to Dizzy and the guys who were pointing at the band in fits of laughter. I didn't know what was happening. I leaned on the tips of my toes to get a view over the wall of people lining the street.

There was Mike. He was dribbling through the band,

testing his own ball handling skills and being a clown. He made a nice spin move on the percussion section and then crossed over on a tuba player who looked like he was going to collapse from heat exhaustion. I began laughing hysterically. Finally, Mike came across the street. "Those tuba players can't cover me." He laughed and we made our way to the courts. With the noise from the parade in the background, we did what we did every day that summer: got ready for our final year of high school basketball.

By the time our senior season rolled around, we were sure that our final chance would bring us the title. That year, we entered the playoffs as the number two seed and cruised right to the state championship game. On the other side of the bracket, top seeded Brooklyn Central held up their end of the bargain. This set up Brooklyn's Backcourt versus Harlem's Hope. Only this time Mike would be in uniform, not a pair of jeans.

Two days before tip-off, Randy Collier, the head coach for UNY, added fuel to an already roaring fire. "I'm very interested in the state championship game this year because of the four guards that are involved. We'll see which pair's better this Thursday. We're gonna try and snag a pair of those kids and put 'em in a UNY uniform."

Thursday arrived. We emerged from our bus on game night accosted by television reporters and photographers. A pair of old headphones covered my ears as I made my way through the traffic and into the locker room. Voices were muted by my music. The world around me was as well. I knew what was at stake; a state championship and a college scholarship.

I put on my battle gear: shorts, a jersey, two wristbands, and a worn pair of size eleven high-tops. I moved to the center of the locker room, beneath the white fluorescent lights that flickered and buzzed. Everyone gathered around me. Pressed in tightly, we looked more like a pile than a circle. Guys were yelling, somebody barked, and then we all began jumping.

I grabbed a pile of hands and shouted, "Who are we?"

In unison, "Forty-four! Forty-four!" The guys shouted the number of our school.

"From where?" I screamed, hopping up and down, spit shooting from my lower lip.

"Harlem! Harlem!" The guys yelled.

"*Who* are we?" I screamed even louder.

With fists in a ball and heads touching one another, the volume grew. "Forty-four! Forty-four!"

Coach Harris put his hands in the pile and began jumping up and down with us. "How we gonna get this done tonight?" he shouted.

The answer came loud and proud, "Together, together, together!" When we ran out of that locker room, we were together in every sense of the word.

I looked around dizzily during warm-ups. A capacity crowd of well over 3,500 fans were packed into Tinsley College arena. The stands looked like an overflowing bag of popcorn. In the mayhem, I noticed a familiar face courtside. University of New York's Coach Collier was perched in a front row seat, sporting his old clipboard and an orange soda.

On my first trip up the floor, James Thomas reminded me of why I disliked him so much. He picked his trash talk up right where he left off a year ago. "Now I know why they call you two guys the Hope Brothers. Every night before you suckers go to sleep, you stay awake and *hope* you don't have to play us." He chuckled to himself. "Your worst nightmare's coming true tonight."

I winked at Thomas and smiled. "Let's do this." I proceeded to cross him up, switching my dribble from left to right and darting past him. My explosiveness caught him off guard. When I made my way into the lane, Walter Randolph cut in front. His vicious foul sent me reeling backward. In desperation, I lofted a shot that kissed off the glass and dropped in. My free throw completed the three-point play.

Adrenaline rushed through my body. I slapped the floor and crouched down into a defensive stance, pulling at my shorts and moving my feet. I had a feeling that Thomas would try to do something to answer my three-point play. He glared at me near half court, dribbling nonchalantly. Suddenly, Thomas woke from his slumber and charged at me. I shuffled back, but he stopped on a dime, leaving me off balance.

Thomas thought he had enough separation for a shot, and last year, he probably would have. This year, my stronger legs regained their balance. He squared his shoulders, ready to launch his jumper. I sprouted into the air like a kangaroo. From three inches above him, I swatted his shot. My authoritative block sent the basketball bouncing toward the other end of the court.

I sprinted after the loose ball. Besides worrying about Thomas catching me, I had to hurry before the rock rolled out of bounds. As I went airborne to save it, I noticed a figure from the corner of my eye. "On your wing," my brother shouted as I sprawled out. I beat Thomas to the ball and slapped it over my left shoulder. From the floor, I saw Mike corral the pass and rise up. His thunderous dunk put us up 5-0.

After the hot start, our team reacted. We swarmed like killer bees, harassing Brooklyn's Backcourt with defensive pressure. With three minutes left until halftime, we led 44 – 29.

That's when Randolph caught fire. On Brooklyn Central's next four possessions he drained three-pointers from everywhere. He swished two from straight away with Mike's hand in his face. His third shot banked home from the same spot, pure luck. The exclamation point rattled in from about ten feet beyond the arc as the halftime buzzer sounded. In the time it took for Mom to grab some peanuts, Randolph had shrunk our lead to three.

The third quarter was a defensive struggle from the start. Mike and I shadowed Thomas and Randolph, forcing them to heave up prayers. Their shots clanked off the rim and the backboard. They'd put up enough bricks to build a fireplace, yet at the close of the third, we led by only five.

Between quarters, Coach Harris demanded that Mike and I take control of the game's offensive tempo. On our first possession Mike took his words to heart, racing down the court with no regard for his body. He slid between defenders recklessly until he crashed head on with gigantic Will Bromwell. At that same moment, Walter Randolph clipped him from behind. It was a Hope sandwich and Bromwell and Randolph were the bread. Mike dropped to the floor as the whistle blew.

He clutched his knee in agony.

Mom stood up with both hands covering her mouth. Our trainer helped my brother to the bench, wrapping his knee in ice. I'd seen that pained expression on Mike's face before. I was sure I'd be finishing this game without him.

After Mike's injury, Brooklyn Central rattled off thirteen straight points.

With five minutes left in our season, we stared down an eight-point deficit. Coach Harris called a time-out, our grasp on a state championship slipping. We formed a semi-circle around him. "Tony, you've got to start looking inside. And Dizzy, shoot the ball when you're open, son! With Mike out we need -"

"I'm right here Coach." Mike stood up, pulling the ice pack from his purple knee. "I'm ready to play."

Coach put his hands on my brother's shoulders. "Are you sure?" He spoke with a proud expression on his face.

"I'm not gonna sit here while we blow our last chance. Let's turn this thing around."

We all breathed a sigh of relief and Dizzy found his old seat on the bench. Mike was back.

I walked out onto the floor with my brother half-limping next to me. The crowd stood, applauding his bravery. Thomas looked over at Mike and smiled. "That leg better be working, Hope." Mike didn't say anything, staring straight ahead.

He walked over to me and whispered, "Feed me the ball, T. We're not losing this game."

In agony, Mike dragged his leg forward and pushed up the floor. When I reached half court, I waited for him and bounced a pass to his side. He caught the ball awkwardly. Nearly losing his balance, he shot from one leg. His jump shot, if you want to call it that, was somehow perfect. The three-pointer tickled nothing but nylon, cutting the lead to five.

Sensing the crowd's enthusiasm Mike urged them on with a pump of his fist. Suddenly his limp was more of a strut. And as James Thomas dribbled up the court, the raucous fans were chanting, "Forty-Four" loudly. We were the underdog, and people love to root for the underdog.

Thomas tossed a pass over to Randolph, who dribbled to his left. Mike was waiting for him, instincts making up for his broken wheel. He slapped the ball away from Randolph. I took off, Thomas blanketing me. Mike saw me break and lofted a balloon pass down court.

The orange rainbow had every eye in the house staring toward the rafters. My head bobbed up and down as I sprinted toward Mike's outlet pass. Both my arms stretched to their limits and the ball landed softly in my hands. Wearing Thomas like a backpack, I rose into the air for a slam. I'd caught him by surprise. I never dunked in games.

I looked down at him from the rim. "Didn't know I could fly, did you?"

From there, my brother and his dark purple knee took over. If anyone in the arena questioned who the best player on that court was, over the next few minutes, Mike gave them the answer. He made his next eight shots to keep *Hope* alive. With thirty seconds remaining we trailed by just a point.

I dribbled the ball patiently as the clock clicked to twenty-five seconds. Managing time at the end of a close game is the truest test of a point guard.

"One shot!" Coach Harris screamed from the sidelines.

I watched the clock, devising a game plan in my head, "Eighteen seconds, Tony. Stay calm. Careful with the ball. Don't show'em where you're going. Find Mike. There he is. He's covered. Get open, Mike. Fifteen seconds left. Come on Mike, get open. All right. Don't panic. Thirteen seconds. Okay, here comes Thomas, he'll try for the steal. Twelve…Eleven! Now go!"

I looked for a way to get Mike the ball. Randolph had him wrapped up like a birthday present. I checked out my other options. Jermaine Smith was covered. Rick Haynes tried to fight through a pick. Juan Rose slipped to the floor. No one had an inch.

With seven seconds remaining I looked toward the hoop. The final shot would be mine. I quickly faked left, then crossed over right, my signature move. Thomas lost a half step. I had a lane! Will Bromwell, the enormous center, came charging at me with his arms raised high.

Four seconds. Fading back, I chucked one up. I thought my high-archer had a chance. But the ball ricocheted off the rim and into the air, a brick. I'd missed the game winner. The giant center positioned himself in front of the basket for the rebound.

Three seconds left. Hands grabbed for the ball that seemed to hang in the air forever. We'd fought hard, but it appeared that once again we'd come up short.

Two seconds. From nowhere, I saw my brother flying toward the pile of hands. His extended left arm hovered above the rim, barely reaching the ball as the clock wound down to one.

I still don't understand how he did it, but somehow his banged up knee propelled him six feet through the air and above the pile beneath the basket. His arm miraculously powered the ball through Bromwell's massive paws, through two other hands that had a grasp, and finally, through the net before the buzzer sounded.

Mike fell to the floor with the ball bouncing next to him. We'd won the state championship!

For twelve guys and Coach Harris, there was no greater sight in the world than seeing my brother dunk home that basketball. We mobbed the court as champions. In the midst of the pile, I jumped on top of my brother, who was laughing and wincing in pain. "We did it, Mike!"

Three days later Coach Collier called, offering two full scholarships to attend the University of New York. Mike and I proudly accepted. Coach gave us this advice, "Stay in shape and out of trouble this summer."

I only wish that Mike had listened.

CHAPTER SEVEN

INVINCIBLE

Three months after winning the state championship against Brooklyn's Backcourt, and thirteen hours before we were supposed to leave Harlem for UNY, I was searching for my brother. That's where this whole story starts, on the night of the chase.

I followed Mike all over Harlem that night. I watched as he hid behind dumpsters to avoid the police. I watched him pass by "Sweet Feet's" house without a second glance. Finally, my pursuit led me to the warehouse, where I heard gunshots.

Nick and Devon sprinted past me on my way to the entrance. They were both holding guns in their hands. I knew these guys weren't role models, but I had no idea they were carrying weapons. Sirens sounded. "Where's Mike?" I screamed through the ruckus. Fleeing like cowards, they didn't answer. Instead, they ran full speed toward the alleyway. Two *police officers gave chase, trailing close behind.*

The front window to the warehouse had been sprayed with bullets. I stepped through piles of broken glass as I moved closer to the door. The sounds of blaring sirens grew louder and louder. I waited for Mike to follow his friends out. I knew if Nick and Devon had just left, he couldn't be far behind. "Mike!" I shouted. "Mike!" I yelled in a panic, hoping he would tap me on the shoulder at any moment.

Another police car arrived on the scene. I watched as Devon was pushed into the back seat in handcuffs. He and Nick had been caught before they'd gotten a block away. Tears rolled down Nick's cheek as he spoke to me, "I'm sorry, T. Mike didn't want any of this." He looked at the warehouse.

I now knew where Mike was. I ran past two policemen who were questioning a female witness. I stepped over another pile of broken glass. My right hand pushed the door open, and I passed through. When I looked down, I saw a face that looked like my own. "Oh my God! Mike!" I screamed, hovering over my brother's body. He'd been shot.

Mike lay still on the floor, barely conscious. "C'mon Mike," I squeezed his hand, feeling nothing in return. "Let's go, Hope, fight! Don't leave me. Fight, Mike!"

An instant later, paramedics were pushing me out of the way and placing Mike onto a stretcher. They stuck him with needles and gave him oxygen. Before I knew it, the ambulance was speeding away toward the hospital with both of us inside.

Mike was tied to machines that I'd only seen in the movies. Something was in his mouth and blood soaked towels covered his wounds. After everything had been hooked into him, I shuffled behind a few of the paramedics and stood above my brother. I reached down and grabbed his hand. "I'm still here bro — still right here. Don't leave, I need you. Fight, Mike!" His eyes moved around in circles like he was looking for something. Finally, they found mine. "I need you."

I looked over at the screen monitoring his barely beating heart. I squeezed his hand a little tighter. What if Mike died? How could I go on living without my wing-man? The next morning we were supposed to be leaving for UNY. We'd stayed out of trouble right up until the last moments.

Just as we pulled up to the front of the emergency room, Mike surprised everyone with an enormous gasp for air. He wasn't giving up. A few paramedics were so surprised, they flinched. When the double doors of the ambulance opened, Mike was rolled out like a tornado. In a flash, he was gone down the hallway and into a room that I wasn't permitted to enter.

On the other side of that door my brother would fight for his life. Our dreams were suddenly unimportant. All that mattered was Mike leaving that room alive. By being at that party he'd made the worst mistake of his life. In those moments of desperation, I realized that I had as well. I should have stopped him.

I was sitting in a dark green chair, hands covering my face when I heard Mom's voice. "Tony, what happened?" She was hysterical. I had never seen my mother cry like that before and I hope I never will again. She hugged me and spoke through tears, "Why did my baby get shot?"

Mom sat down in the green chair. I started to speak,

but couldn't. I didn't want to tell her what happened. Mom had worked so hard to keep us out of trouble. Dad left when Mom was pregnant and the only thing that kept our family from crumbling was the strength of our mother. But that night, I saw something different in her face. I knew that at least for a while, she couldn't be strong anymore. If she lost her son tonight, I wondered if she would ever be strong again. "How's he doing, Tony? Just tell me he's gonna be okay."

I wasn't sure if I even believed it, but I knew in those moments something had to be said. "He's gonna be fine, Mom. I know it." I had to offer her this hope. "He took a deep breath just as we came into the hospital. I saw it. He'll be all right."

Mom was trying to calm herself. "Where did he get shot?"

I couldn't look at her. "In the back. I guess Nick and Devon had some enemies at the party. Those guys started shooting. Nick and Devon shot back. Mike was running away, and he got hit - " Tears started rolling down my face. "He got shot three times, Mom."

Neither one of us said much after that. I sat on the floor while Mom stared at the wall blankly, squeezing my hand every so often. Five hours had passed since we arrived at the hospital. The waiting was unbearable. At any moment, doctors would appear and tell me whether my brother was dead or alive.

Mom always told us how precious life was. There are consequences for every action. In the time it takes to cough, sneeze, flinch, burp, step, chew, swallow, smile – one second – poof, it can all be over. A night of partying with the wrong *crowd can turn into disaster. You can end up with three bullets lodged in your back, fighting to stay alive like Mike. Life is a delicate egg, and if you treat it any other way, you'll end up scrambled.*

Suddenly, the door to Mike's room swung open. Mom and I leaped to our feet and walked toward a black doctor in her early thirties. She had a strange expression on her face. I tried to read it, but couldn't. She approached us and removed her mask. "Mike is alive and is now in stable condition."

I hugged my mother. "My baby's okay. He's okay." Mom repeated this again and again. Mike Hope had stayed alive.

After hugging Mom for a minute I looked over my shoulder and noticed the doctor still standing there. She had something else to say. My sense of relief was put on hold. "Doctor?" I looked at her anxiously. "Is my brother all right or not?"

She cleared her throat, "It was a miracle that Mike survived. He took three shots in the back from close range." The doctor was rattled. "Two of the bullets that entered Mike's back missed his vital organs by centimeters, that's the only reason he's still alive. But the third bullet - " She took a deep breath, "The third bullet hit Mike in his spinal chord. I'm sorry, we did all we could. He's paralyzed from the waist down."

Right in the middle of the word "paralyzed," Mom dropped to the floor. She wasn't crying anymore, she was numb. The doctor continued, "He needs to rest for a few hours, then you can see him. I'm so sorry."

I guided Mom up and helped her into a chair. Mean-

while, I was pacing around the room. "Paralyzed from the waist down." I kept replaying those words over and over again in my head. "Paralyzed from the waist down." Despite everything we'd been through, all the training, all the dreaming, UNY, NBA plans, it all came down to those words, "Paralyzed from the waist down."

Suddenly, I couldn't stop crying. My best friend, my shadow, would never walk again. In fate's cruelest twist, basketball had been taken away from Mike Hope. Nobody loved that game like my brother.

After hours of waiting, a nurse informed us that Mike was awake and ready for visitors. "Mom, you go ahead first. I'll go after." She kissed me on the head and walked into the room. I sat back down on the floor, trying to figure out what I would say to my brother.

I brought my knees close to my chest and wrapped my arms around them. I hadn't sat like that since I was a little kid. I closed my eyes. Suddenly, I was on a hardwood floor in a New York Pride jersey. Two defenders darted toward me. I picked up my dribble and threw a cross-court pass that Mike caught in stride. I watched him soar to the hoop and hammer home a spectacular dunk.

When I opened my eyes, I didn't hear the screams of excited fans. I was still in the hospital waiting room. My brother was paralyzed, and the sounds of my mother crying shook the sterile hallways.

About twenty minutes later Mom went to a nearby room to lie down. She looked exhausted. A freckled nurse waved me in. "Your brother's been asking for you." I stood up from my *seat cautiously. Before I entered the room I stopped in the door-way to gather my thoughts. Mike was staring out the window, lying on his back perfectly still. I wondered what he was think-ing. When I was a few feet away he turned his head toward me. "Where've you been? Scared to see me?" Mike knew me bet-ter than I knew myself.*

I spoke awkwardly, "No, I just – I wanted to give Mom a chance to – you know. How are you?"

"I got shot in the back three times, Tony. I'm not doing that well."

I'd thought about what I would say to my brother for the past three hours, but all I came up with was a stupid ques-tion. "Does it hurt?"

Suddenly, Mike's eyes welled up with tears. He looked scared as he spoke, "I don't know, Tony, I can't feel any-thing."

When Mike said that I burst into tears, "Mike, what did you do?" I yelled at him. "What did you do to yourself?" I began crying on his shirt, leaning my face into his stomach as his hands palmed over the top of my head.

"Easy, I'm all right. I'm still talking to you, aren't I? I'm not dead. It's still me in here." I had to get control of myself. I pulled up a seat next to him. He spoke in a serious tone, "Listen T, I'm done with basketball. I'm done with walk-ing to the store, taking showers, even standing up. I know this. But I still feel lucky. I should be dead." He paused, "Do you know why I'm still alive?"

I shook my head. He continued, "I've been given this second chance because you need me. That's what you told me when I was lying there in the ambulance. That's what I kept telling myself. That's why I kept fighting."

Mike moved his head around on the bed, searching for a comfortable spot. I sensed his frustration and propped up his pillow. "Thanks." He wasn't finished yet. "Tony, you're Harlem's Hope now. You're my hope. Take us to the top. Just like we planned."

Although my timing wasn't right, there was something I had to get off my chest. I would only scold my brother once and then I'd never say anything again. "I'm so happy that you're alive. But I'm so upset, Mike. You said you'd never leave me again." I paused. "I can't understand why you went to that party. You knew Devon and Nick were looking for trouble, everybody did."

"I know, Tony. I blew it. I should never have gone." Mike stared at me for a minute. "I guess I thought I was invincible."

I know he wanted me to tell him I was ready to take on life without him. I wasn't. "It shouldn't have happened like this. It was supposed to be you and me. How am I supposed to play without you? I was never the great player, you were always making great plays." I laid my head back down on Mike's stomach.

His voice deepened, "Tony. Look at me, this is important." I picked my head up. "You're gonna be a star." He paused, out of breath. "And some day you're gonna have a moment where everything will get clear, and you'll realize this — you've always been a great player, always."

I put my head back on his chest. I was sure that day

would never come. Mike wanted me to continue our dream. But sitting there in that room, nothing seemed important to me anymore.

CHAPTER EIGHT

THE FARMER

The morning Mike came home from the hospital we had pancakes. Mom and I sat around the kitchen table in an awkward quiet as Mike wheeled himself over. The wheels on Mike's chair banged into the legs of the table repeatedly as he tried to adjust his position so that he could reach his plate. Mom looked over at me. "Tony, help your brother."

Mike bumped the table a few more times, unfamiliar with his chair. I started to stand up, but he didn't want my help. "Sit down, T. I can do this. You have to let me do this stuff." Mom and I tried not to watch Mike fumble with his chair. He bumped the table again, this time his fork dropped to the floor. I started to stand, but, "Tony, sit down. I can use my spoon."

I stared at the fork lying on the floor. I didn't know how to act. Everything inside me wanted to grab that fork, hand it to Mike, push in his chair, cut his pancakes, anything I could do to help. Instead, I grabbed a blueberry pancake and dropped it onto my plate. An eerie silence overtook the room. The only noise we could hear was the creaking of Mike's chair as he tried to get comfortable at the table. From the corner of my eye, I glanced at him in his wheelchair. Sweat beads dripped off his forehead. When our eyes met, I glanced back at my pancakes. Watching the guy who used to move through life with such grace, bump into tables and lose his balance, was heartbreaking.

It's a strange thing being brothers. You grow to be an extension of one another. That's why in those moments I felt like I knew exactly what Mike was feeling. His frustration was contagious. I stared at the stack of blueberry pancakes, unable to eat. The shape of Mike's wheelchair and the shape of the table left him about three feet from his plate. Mike reached forward, unable to get to his food. After a few exhausting moments, he gave up, throwing his spoon down and rolling himself into the living room awkwardly.

Mom looked over at me, raising her eyebrows, encouraging me to speak. I didn't know what to say. Mike broke the silence from the other room. "Tony, what are you still doing here? You were supposed to leave for school two weeks ago. If you want to help me, go to college. You've gotta give me some time to get used to this." If Mike could still move his legs, I was sure he would have pushed me out the front door. As he was, he just stared me down.

That night I boarded the Six train and left Harlem. Next stop, The University of New York. I was scared of facing life without Mike, but I couldn't bear to upset him further.

An hour later, I lugged a green duffle bag through a crowded corridor in Van Patten Hall, my college dormitory and new home. The bag dragged on the dirty floor, and a kid on a skateboard hopped over it as he passed. Loud music rattled the walls around me. The sounds were different than the sounds I'd grown up with. The people seemed different too.

I unlocked the door to Room 18, a small place with plain furniture. Inside, there was two of everything. Two beds, two desks, two chairs, and two lamps on opposite sides of the room. I dropped my bag onto the left bed and sat in my new chair, quietly staring at tan walls. The bed across from me was littered with a gym bag and a couple of CDs I'd never heard of.

When the door swung open a moment later, a tall, thin, goofy looking white guy stumbled into the room. He extended his hand toward mine. "Are you Tony?" he asked.

I shook his hand. "Yeah, I'm Tony."

"I'm Josh, Josh Gibson. My friends call me Gibby. I guess we're roommates. I've got allergies, so I took the bed farthest from the window. Is that cool?"

My head nodded reflexively. I was barely listening to what Josh was saying.

He continued trying to make conversation. "So, you run the point? I play two guard." He paused. "I'm not Mike but - "

"These rooms are tiny." I quickly changed the subject, unwilling to discuss my brother. Mike was headline news in New York and everyone seemed to have a comment.

I turned my back to Josh and began unpacking my bags,

avoiding further dialogue. I had never shared a room with anyone except my brother, and he always slept near the window. Now *I* was by the window. Everything was off. And this Josh guy was annoying. Every time he opened his mouth he was asking me a question about something I didn't want to talk about. We had nothing in common. He was from some farm in Pennsylvania. I was born and raised in Harlem. What did I know about a farm?

This was gonna be a long year. We weren't going to be friends, and I didn't want to spend the year pretending. "Listen Gibson, you keep yourself on that side of the room and me and you will be all right." Josh's face dropped. Our conversation was over.

When I went to bed that night, I stared at the ceiling wondering if I had made a huge mistake by coming to UNY and leaving Mike. Josh interrupted my thoughts, speaking in short whispers from across the dark room, "Tony, you awake?" I pretended to be asleep. "Tony?" I wouldn't answer. He continued anyway. "I know I'm a farm boy and you're from the city, but I'd like to be friends. We could be good friends, me and you." I didn't want to make friends. I wanted my brother. *He* should have been lying in that bed, not some farmer. I remained silent. A moment later, I closed my eyes and went to sleep.

Basketball practice the next morning was awful. After warm-ups and a short meeting, Coach Collier ordered the freshman to scrimmage against last year's starters. Josh played on my team along with three other newcomers. Surprisingly, Gibson was a solid player. His goofy manner masked fluid athleticism and a jump shot that was as sweet as candy. I couldn't help but imagine how good our freshman class would have been with Mike on the team.

I was completely out of sync during that scrimmage, turning the ball over again and again. With the upperclassmen leading by four, I casually dribbled into the front court. There was one defender directly in front of me and I felt another closing in quickly from my left. With everyone trying to earn a starting spot, defensive intensity ran high. As for me, I was numb to the entire situation.

The defense closed in. "On your wing, T. On your wing if you need me." I heard Mike's voice and threw a perfect pass to my right. I watched the ball bounce twice on the hardwood floor before sailing out of bounds. No one was there. Mike was in Harlem.

Coach Collier pulled a cigarette from his mouth and began coughing violently. His southern drawl rang out. "Hey Hope! Are you with us here? You all right, kid?" I didn't answer, staring at the sidelines, dazed. "Hallaway! Run the point! Hope, take a breather."

I walked over to the bench where I sat staring at the number 44 that I'd written on my sneakers. Mike's number. Coach Collier came over and sat down next to me. I perked up and looked him in the eyes as he spoke, "You've gotta get that head screwed on straight, Hope. I'm sorry about your brother, I really am. But this team needs you. You've got to find your game out there, without Mike." He patted me on the back. "Come back in when you're ready, Tony."

I never returned to the floor that day.

The first few weeks of school were terrible. I was having trouble concentrating in class, and I'd barely spoken a word to my roommate. But the thing that troubled me most was that basketball was no longer fun. In the darkest hours of my life I had no one to turn to. I couldn't burden Mike with my problems.

Anger, frustration, and bitterness grew from my silence. I was ready to stand up and walk the fifteen miles home. Wherever I went, the sounds of Harlem played in my head. Suddenly, being one of the guys that hung around the Jungle and spoke about what could have been, didn't seem that bad. I began to wonder how I ever could have left Mike.

One Thursday, after another bad test grade, I realized that I was sitting in the wrong place. Nothing was going my way at UNY. The time had come to go home. When class let out I started my jog back to Van Patten Dormitory to pack my stuff.

As I turned the key to enter my dorm room loud music blared from inside. *My* music. Josh was sitting on the edge of my bed, bouncing his head to the beat and glancing through my CD case. He didn't even hear the door open when I came in. All the emotions running through my body erupted as I yanked the stereo's chord out of the wall.

I grabbed Josh by the shirt. "What did I tell you, Gibson? What did I say about my stuff?" There was a pause for a few seconds as I stared hard at Josh. Fear radiated from his body, but it did nothing to lessen my anger. "Answer me, Gibson! Didn't I tell you to keep off my stuff? Didn't I?"

Josh pushed my hands away from his shirt and looked

the other way. "You're crazy, Hope. You know that?" He paused. "You haven't tried with me since the moment I got here."

I was confused. "Tried what?"

"Did you ever try to give me a chance? The answer's no." Josh tossed my CD case onto my bed. "Keep your CDs."

Josh had me rattled. I sat down and put my hands on my head. I owed him an explanation. "The only reason I'm here is because UNY wanted my brother. He was the best ballplayer in the country last year. Recruited from everywhere. We were a package deal." I paused. "But he got shot — now he can't walk." I wasn't sure I could finish my sentence. "I'm sorry for not giving you a chance. I just miss playing ball with my brother."

My saddened tone changed the angry expression on Josh's face to one of compassion. "I know all about your brother, T. I'm sorry."

There was more I had to say, "This room was supposed to be for Mike and me. This was supposed to be our dream. But that dream's over. I'm leaving here tonight." I began emptying the contents of my drawers into the green duffle bag.

After I had filled the bag about halfway, Josh turned it upside down. T-shirts, boxers and socks tumbled to the floor. "I can't let you leave, Tony. I've spent my whole life trying to get here and I know you have too. I can't let you throw all of that away. I'm sure if your brother was here he'd tell you the same thing."

Josh was trying to do a good thing, but my mind was already made up. "You're not my brother. I'm leaving." I began re-packing.

He tumbled my bag upside down again. "Maybe you don't understand. I'm going to play in the NBA. If you leave, that might not happen."

"My leaving doesn't affect you. Why do you care, anyway, Gibson?" I pushed Josh aside. "Now move, you're blocking my way to the closet."

He bounced back into place. "I came here on a mission. I have a dream, the same way you do. In the last four weeks I've come to realize that you and I are the two best players in this freshman class. Without you, it's just me out there. You know what that means? When I'm a senior, the NBA scouts aren't even gonna look my way, because UNY isn't gonna be a team to look at." Josh pleaded with me. "You're a great point guard. And I can score. Maybe not the same way your brother could, but I got here for a reason too. You *haven't* given me a chance." Josh spoke with so much feeling in his voice, he reminded me of Mike. "Let's go down to the courts, the lights are on until ten."

I started to smile. I hadn't smiled in a long time. "You wanna be my wing man, farmer? All right, I'll play one game, but you better be good." I dropped my duffle bag, laced up my high-tops and put on a practice jersey.

We walked down to the courts together. Josh bounced the ball the entire way, telling me about life on the farm. He talked about waking up at sunrise and shooting baskets on a hoop in the middle of some cornfields. I told him that I'd never even seen cornfields.

Then he started talking about life without a dad, and

how his Mom worked two jobs just to pay the bills. His account of growing up with a single parent sounded just like mine. As he spoke, I found myself finishing his sentences. We had more in common than I thought. I even told him about something I never talked about, *my* dad. He left Mom when she was pregnant with Mike and me. Like Josh, I didn't hold a grudge. Both of our moms had done great all by themselves.

By the time we were a block away from the court, I was telling Josh all about the Jungle and basketball in Harlem. He couldn't believe my stories. "You guys play five on five every day? Back home, I can't even find someone to rebound for me."

When we reached the court we saw two familiar faces. Billy Cunningham and Jason Jackson were playing a night game of H-O-R-S-E. They were the senior guards on our team, the same guys that Josh and I would be backing up once the season started. We said hello, and immediately Josh challenged them to a game of two-on-two. Billy and Jason wanted to split the teams up, "making it fair" as Cunningham said in a cocky voice. We insisted on playing young guys versus old, game to fifteen by ones.

Although we were juiced, Cunningham and Jackson were half-asleep. The game started, and Cunningham dribbled the ball at the top of the key, telling Jackson a funny story about some girl he'd met at a party. Jackson made weak cuts to the basket through fits of laughter. Cunningham's tale continued as he nailed a jumper over me. Then another. Then another, all the while detailing his story about the girl. This guy wasn't taking me seriously and I understood why. I hadn't proven myself once at UNY and now I was being completely embarrassed.

Cunningham wouldn't shut up. "So then, she tells her friend Holly that - "

I was done with his stupid story. I swiped the ball from his hands and bounced a pass to Josh who launched a shot from about thirty feet. Swish!

I looked over at Cunningham and smiled. "Three-one. Is story time over yet?"

Suddenly, I was dribbling intensely, and doing something I hadn't done in the five weeks since my brother had been paralyzed. I was having fun on a basketball court.

Cunningham and Jackson never found a flow during that game. They talked back and forth, and threw up brick after brick. On the other hand, Josh and I played well together, and took a surprising fourteen-six lead on the seniors.

On game point, I had Cunningham confused. I dribbled forward, than backward, side to side, and behind my back. The senior lunged for the ball helplessly. Jackson saw a chance at a steal and came over to apply the double team. Instinctively, I threw the ball toward the rim. Usually when I was trapped, I would toss a prayer toward the rim. Somehow, Mike would grab it and score. But with Mike back in Harlem, I was sure I'd turned the ball over. I watched my pass float to the hoop and toward the out of bounds line.

Without my brother, things would never be the same on a basketball court. Errant passes around the rim would no longer be assists. I began to doubt myself, wondering again, was I really a playmaker or had Mike just made great plays?

Then, Gibby, a six-foot-five twig, rose up from the baseline. In mid-air, he caught the ball, and slammed it home with two hands.

I raised my arms in triumph. I *was* a playmaker, and the farmer could play.

CHAPTER NINE

STEPPING INTO THE LIGHT

Mom didn't raise quitters. I decided to stay at UNY.

My freshman season began a week after our two on two trouncing of Cunningham and Jackson. Our first game was against Rhode Island State's Flying Fish, a team that hadn't been ranked among the top twenty-five since I was three years old. We entered the game ranked seventh in the nation, fully expecting a rout. Yet somehow, the Fish hung around. With ten minutes remaining in the second half, they trailed by only four.

Cunningham ran the show exclusively during those first thirty minutes. But even the most finely conditioned point guard had trouble playing an entire game without a break. When I noticed him gasping for air I glanced over at Coach Collier. He looked torn. Play the freshman or let the senior run out of gas? Coach ran his fingers through his thinning hair for a few tension filled moments. Finally, he caved in. "Hope, get in there for Cunningham."

I tore off my warm-ups frantically, tripping over hanging pant legs on my way to the scorer's table. From the moment I stepped onto the court, I noticed something completely different about college basketball. The game at the Division I level was played at a frantic pace. If you blinked, you were beaten.

I dribbled to half court and passed the ball over to our power forward, Vance Wilson. I guess I'd telegraphed my delivery, because the ball was tipped and intercepted by a Rhode Island State defender. He went coast to coast for an easy lay-up. Clinging to a two-point lead, Coach Collier signaled for a timeout. As I approached the sidelines, he looked away from me in disgust, searching down the bench for Cunningham. "You ready to get back in there, Billy?"

After one trip down the floor, Cunningham was back in the game and I was back on the bench. My costly error erased the little confidence Coach had in me. That turnover was the first of many in an ugly second half filled with follies. The final score wasn't a sight to behold either, Rhode Island State 86, UNY 78.

Our season had opened disastrously. Needless to say, the next few practices brought an added intensity. My rude introduction to college basketball was about to get downright nasty. An East Coast road trip loomed.

The first of these tough games was against the University of Trenton Pitbulls. They were ranked thirteenth in the nation. Playing in front of their rabid fans inflated an already difficult challenge. The Kennel, as it was called, was one of the loudest arenas in college basketball. UNY had been beaten handily on the last three trips to Trenton.

When I entered the gym for warm-ups, I was overwhelmed. Being on the floor was like being a fish in an overcrowded glass bowl. Inside, bottled chaos awoke. Cameras shot from every angle. Television announcers combed their hair and reviewed statistics. Cheerleaders flipped. Coaches paced, gripping clipboards tightly. We tried to look and act confident, pretending not to watch the Pitbulls as they pretended not to watch us. And then there was the crowd. At Trenton, twenty thousand screaming fans packed the Kennel draped in Pitbull black and red. They chewed on dog bones, barked obscenities, and howled predictions of our demise.

When warm-ups ended, I found my seat. The twenty thousand maniacs bounced up and down as the whistle blew to open play. I hated my view from the bench.

The Pitbulls dominated the first half, backing taunts from their cocky fans. Trenton's precise defense limited our clean looks at the basket. We couldn't get anything going and trailed by eleven, 45-34 at the break.

Halftime hardly cooled the Pitbulls. And when their seven-foot center, Steve House, buried his first four shots after intermission, we knew we were in serious trouble. House's eight points bolstered their advantage to nineteen.

Cunningham dribbled up the court patiently, trying to slow the speedy pace. He dribbled left, around a sophomore point guard who neglected to move his feet. The Pitbull pup lunged for the ball and poked Cunningham in the eye. The defender's finger was about an inch deep in Cunningham's pupil. Billy dropped to the floor, both hands covering the right side of his face in agony. As our trainer led him off the court, he squirmed in obvious pain.

After my miscue against Rhode Island State, I thought junior shooting guard C.J. Katz would step in for Cunningham. Coach checked down the bench, searching for something, anything, to ignite his squad. "Hope, Gibson, get over here!" When Josh and I stood up, some of the Pitbull players smirked, assuming Coach Collier had given up. In front of a packed house, with the season only a week old, two skinny freshmen stepped into the light.

We approached Coach. He shouted over the raucous crowd, "Okay boys, you're the future of this team. Show us something."

Josh and I tapped the top of the scorer's table, checking ourselves into the game. I bent down and touched the number 44 on my sneakers just before Vance Wilson inbounded the ball to me. I threw a pass to Josh, who was hounded by a bigger and stronger defender. Intimidated, he threw the hot potato back out to me. Dribbling to my right, I waited for someone to get open. The defense reacted to every glance I shot at my teammates. I couldn't find a seam anywhere. By the time I tossed another pass to Josh, the shot clock had expired. My second turnover in two college possessions.

Coach Collier peered over at Cunningham, who held an ice pack over his eye. This time, I couldn't be replaced. Beads of sweat formed on Coach's oversized forehead. He faked confidence, clapping his hands. "Let's go guys, we're fine. Focus now!"

The Pitbulls' point guard dished to his right after crossing half court. Josh lunged with his arms, cutting off the passing lane. He stole control of the ball and dribbled down the floor with one defender between himself and the basket. When he reached the free-throw line he stopped short and pulled a jumper. Two points.

We were so excited that on the ensuing trip up the floor, we broke down defensively, leaving Andy Fox a wide open look at a lay up. A stroke of luck spit his shot off the rim and at my chest. I started the break, ball by my side, clear sailing to the basket. But Fox hustled back, jumping into me as I rose to the hoop. His foul knocked both of us to the floor. My knees hit the wood bluntly, followed by the palms of my hand. That pain quickly subsided when I watched the ball dance on the rim and drop into the hoop. Stepping up to the line, I swished a free throw to cut Trenton's lead to fourteen.

Whether from his failed lay up or head first crash landing, Andy Fox was shaken. As our defense applied a full court press, he panicked and carelessly inbounded the ball off Steve House's left foot. I picked up the errant pass and fed Josh, who was camped beyond the three-point line. His shot was perfect. The lead was back to eleven. Trenton State was coming unglued.

During the next ten minutes we were awesome. Led defensively by Philadelphia's Finest, Leroy Hill, and his five blocked shots, we cut the lead to two. Every time a Pitbull found a crease in our defense, the six-eleven sophomore from Philly was there to seal the lane with an emphatic block. Offensively, Josh and I were raining threes. I even caught Coach pumping his fist after one of Gibby's baskets.

With three minutes left, I shuffled in front of the Pitbulls' Jeff Cass. He waved his hands at half court, directing his teammates behind me. I paid close attention to his passing lanes, back pedaling away from Jeff in anticipation. When he noticed the separation, he stepped up and buried a shot from four feet beyond the three-point line. Cass had called his own number. I never saw it coming.

Down by five with a minute-thirty remaining, we faced a critical possession. I dribbled up court quickly. The clock was my enemy, ticking closer and closer to triple zeroes. At the three-point line, I panicked, chucking up a prayer. With the game on the line, I'd made a terrible decision. Unless a strong gust of wind carried the ball toward the hoop, this one was way short. My shot barely nipped the front rim and dove into the largest pair of hands on the floor. Thank goodness for Leroy Hill! He held the rebound high above the defense and dropped in a pretty three-foot hook shot.

With fifty-five seconds remaining, Trenton's Jeff Cass pushed the ball up the floor. I was in his hip pocket like loose change. There was no way he was going to shoot again. Uncomfortable, Cass passed the rock to his back-court mate, Dante Adams. Josh coaxed Adams into launching a quick jumper that smacked iron. Leroy Hill roared as he collected another rebound and handed me the ball.

I zig-zagged through defenders and streaked toward the basket. Three points down. Forty-seven seconds left, forty-six. I leaped into a crowd. Two lanky Pitbull defenders went airborne to thwart my shot. I wasn't going to float the ball over these trees. Instead, I spun in mid-air, shuttling a pass to Leroy who worked his magic again, banking home a short hook.

Thirty seconds remained as Jeff Cass entered the front-court. I fouled him immediately. He made one of his free throws and we trailed by two with twenty-nine seconds remaining.

Coach Collier raised his pointer finger in the air. "One shot. Philadelphia," he demanded. "Philadelphia" was the play we'd practiced for this exact situation. Leroy Hill moved into the low block. We were ready to execute. I zipped a pass to Josh in the corner. Fifteen seconds. Gibby secured a passing lane. His bounce pass landed in Leroy's hands. Right away the big man drew a double team. Nine seconds. Leroy pump-faked, but no one budged. The play was broken. He passed the ball back to me at the top of the key. Five seconds. I dribbled twice and bumped Cass to create some space. Two seconds. I jumped backward and released a shot. As I let the ball go, Cass slapped my wrist. The shot rimmed out but the referee noticed the contact. His whistle blew, directing me to the foul line.

With a line of zeroes on the clock, I had to make a pair of free throws to force overtime. I stepped to the line for the first. My hands were dripping with sweat. Thousands of faces and waving arms distracted me from behind the backboard. I went through my pre-shot routine: three dribbles, quick closing of the eyes, visualize the ball dropping through the hoop, take a look at the rim, release and follow through.

The first shot was perfect. I knew it the second I let go, all net.

The chubby referee grabbed the ball. "Timeout, Trenton State." They'd purposely called that timeout to upset my rhythm.

I jogged over to the bench. My teammates stood in a semicircle around me and placed their hands on the top of my head. Coach Collier spoke. "Okay, five minutes of overtime after Tony makes this shot. We win that, then we grub. Burgers or pizza?" Everyone chuckled at his comment. His joke relaxed me, if just for the moment.

The whistle blew and I walked to the free throw line. The ref tossed me the ball. Holding the game in my shaking hands, I dribbled three times, shut my eyes, opened them, and focused on the rim. "Release, follow through." I repeated this in my head. "Release, follow through."

I released, but didn't follow through. The line drive hit the front of the rim and dropped to the floor. I stood alone as my teammates left the court. We'd come three inches short of overtime. Imagine watching your favorite glass fall off the dinner table. Now, multiply that sense of helplessness by a hundred. That was how I felt on that deserted free throw line. The crowd stood celebrating their team's victory. I had my chance to quiet them but missed.

After the way I'd played during our comeback, I was certain I would be a starter. Yet when we ran drills the next day, Cunningham, eye patch and all, was still with the starting team. I learned something that afternoon. A freshman on Coach Collier's team was about as important as the towel boy.

I sat on some of the nicest benches around that season. Although I learned a great deal about the game, I was itching to be a star. With Cunningham nearing graduation, my opportunity was just around the corner.

Our season ended with a first round loss to Western State in the college championship tournament. I sat quietly in the locker room after the game. Coach Collier and I were the last two left in the building. He snapped a telling comment my way before leaving. "Hope, be ready to run the point next season. You're our guy."

He closed the door behind him. I'd be ready.

CHAPTER TEN

FROM SCRATCH

I returned to Harlem for the summer and dropped my green duffle just inside the front door. I'd seen Mike a few times during my freshman year, but for the most part, school and basketball had kept me from my brother. By the time I arrived home, it occurred to me that Mike had spent close to a year sitting in his wheelchair. Although I tried to imagine what that must have felt like, I couldn't.

Our life had been split in half, and for the first time, we met new experiences alone. While I was going through my first year of collegiate basketball, Mike had started his uphill journey, living life without the use of his legs.

Mom, our quiet hero, made his new life a bit easier by rearranging the apartment. Before Mike's injury there was stuff all over the place. Plants sat on the floor, an end table leaned against the couch, and at least two pairs of sneakers were always somewhere on the carpet. But when I came home after that first summer, everything had changed. There was no clutter on the floor anymore, nothing to get caught in Mike's wheels.

I watched him move around the apartment with the same grace he once walked with. He grabbed my bag from in front of the door, carrying it down the hallway. A year later, he was moving with confidence, his old cockiness restored. I followed him into our bedroom.

"What did you do to this place?" I was staring at a clean room that barely resembled the mess I'd left.

My brother, once the sloppiest guy in the world, had become a neat freak. The beds were made perfectly, laundry had miraculously found its way into the basket, all the drawers were closed, and even the smell was fresh, like a furniture store or something. Aside from that, our room had turned into a gym. Weights lined the sides of the walls in columns. Barbells were in neat rows by the foot of Mike's bed. And as for Mike himself, his upper body resembled that of a professional wrestler, not a nineteen-year-old in a wheelchair.

I picked up a weight. "Do you lift these?" I asked, barely able to do it myself.

He lifted the weight with ease and did a few curls. "Not bad, huh?"

"Not bad." I glanced around the walls in our room. There were articles pinned everywhere. I leaned in closer. Each article described some sort of miracle. One was the story of a blind man who regained his sight after being kicked in the head by a horse. Another described a kid who'd been in a coma for four years and miraculously awoke. The title of the article was,

"Miracles Happen All the Time." Mike had it circled in blue. Finally, I came to the article at the center of his display. This one detailed the story of a woman who'd fully recovered from paralysis. The picture showed her training with weights in her tiny apartment. Mike had highlighted sections throughout the article. "These articles are great. So this stuff really happens, huh?" I read on about the woman who regained use of her legs. "Doctor said she'd never walk again."

Mike wheeled himself closer to me. "I don't believe in never, T."

I turned toward him. "Where'd you get all these?"

"At school. I've been spending a lot of time reading in the library." After Mike's injury, he elected not to attend the University of New York alongside me. Life had altered that path. Instead, he attended Harlem College, where he wheeled himself every morning.

"How you doing in school?" I asked. "Second semester go as well as the first?"

Mike smiled. "I'm a studious student, T. You wouldn't believe it. Been reading all these books," he held up a huge stack, "I must read two a week."

"What about hoops? Do you want to — "

He spoke through my words. "I don't think so, T."

"Let me ask at least. Do you want to come down to the courts with me?"

Mike shook his head and smiled. "I knew you were going to ask me that."

"We can go down to that hoop over by Dizzy's place. It'll be fun."

"I don't know, T."

I grabbed a basketball from the corner of the room and fired it at Mike. He caught it without flinching, the sound made a pop. Palming the ball in his right hand, he closed his eyes, contorting his upper body like he was in mid-air about to make a lay-up. He opened his eyes and tossed the ball back to me. "I'll go watch you shoot." Just holding that ball was enough to convince Mike.

We got there a few minutes later and I began firing away. The basket was set on uneven gravel behind Dizzy's building. There were no nets and the rim bent forward slightly, making it hard to find a rhythm. With the Jungle and the Park in the same neighborhood, people rarely shot around here. That's why I knew this would be a good place to go. Mike would be uncomfortable with everyone watching him.

While I shot, he collected rebounds, talking about life in Harlem without me. I tried to describe the speed of college basketball to Mike. I told him about UNY and Gibby too. He'd watched every minute Josh and I had played on television, all eighteen of them. I mentioned that Coach Collier had assured me that I'd be the starting point guard. He was excited for me.

I bricked one off the rim and Mike gave chase near a faded out-of-bounds line. He got a little fired up, moving himself over to the ball swiftly before it touched the stripe. After he had tracked it down, he threw a pass toward the basket. I rose up, grabbed the rock, and slammed it through the crooked rim. For a short moment, we were playing together again.

I made a few in a row and passed the ball to Mike four feet from the basket. After spinning the leather in his hands, he threw it toward the rim. His shot bounced off the glass and in.

"Nice shot. Try one from a little farther out." I said.

With some confidence now, he rolled to the top of the key, where I tossed him the pill. Mike leaned forward and took his shot. It was on line, but came up short, barely touching the front iron and dropping to the concrete. I grabbed the rebound and passed to Mike again. "Try another one."

His expression changed as he passed the ball back to me. "Nah, you go ahead. I'll rebound."

When my brother had his legs to support his jump shot, he never hit front iron. Watching Mike Hope come up short almost broke my heart that day. When we left the courts, I tried not to look shaken. Mike wasn't fooled. "I know what you're thinking, but don't. There's more to my life than throwing an orange ball through a rim. I'm happy, Tony." *He* was the one in the wheelchair, cheering *me* up. And that's when I realized something, Mike had only come to the courts because I begged him. He didn't need basketball anymore.

July turned into August, and once again, my time in Harlem was over. A week prior to the first practice of my sophomore season, I received a terrifying phone call that really shook me. Coach Collier had suffered a heart attack. Cigarette smoking nearly took his life. Although he survived the massive attack, he was forced to retire. The stress of coaching was too much of a strain for his tar-covered heart.

Could I be facing another season of bench warming? Coach Collier had assured me that I was the starting point guard. What if our new coach had other ideas?

When I arrived at the first scheduled practice, Josh

greeted me at center court biting the nails on his shooting hand. "There's some guy sitting up in the bleachers, T. I think he's our new coach." There had been no announcement as to who would take over the program. Paranoia consumed us. Josh spit a nail onto the court. "Coach Morris told this guy we were starters, right?"

"Of course," I answered, not believing what I said.

In the middle of our conversation I heard a voice. A tall black man hidden in the bleachers blew his whistle. "Nobody takes a shot until we stretch." Everybody looked up at the strange man blankly, his face disguised by dim lighting. "Stretch!" he commanded.

Everyone dropped to the floor. We'd just met our new coach.

We stretched our quads, loosened our necks, and made sure to pull on our hamstrings. All the while, the mystery man edged closer. Weak light shone down from the rafters as he reached the court. I tapped Josh on the shoulder excitedly, "Is that who I think it is?"

Entranced, Josh spoke. "Oh my gosh, that's 'Sweet Feet' Williams!"

The legend had traded in his high tops for a coach's whistle. He strutted to center court. We all stopped stretching. In disbelief, we watched his every move. Lamar Williams was standing in our gym and, by the look of things, he was our new head coach. 'Sweet Feet' didn't need introductions, but went ahead anyway. "I'm Lamar Williams, your new coach." Whispers flooded the gym. Lamar's deep voice grew louder, "You can call me Coach or Coach Williams, whichever you'd like."

Leroy Hill spoke from the back of a circle that engulfed Coach Williams. "What about 'Sweet Feet?'"

Coach chuckled along with the rest of us, "Sweet Feet's retired. It's Coach or Coach Williams, okay?" His smile faded. "And on this court, my feet aren't moving, yours are." He tried to make eye contact with everyone in the circle. "In the next three weeks, the only thing *sweet* is gonna be the moment practice ends. I'm gonna work you guys harder than you've ever worked. And before this season ends, I'm gonna teach you what it takes to win. Some of you may already think you know how to win." He grabbed my hand, staring at my fingers. He did the same to Josh, then to a couple others. "I don't see any championship rings, though." He pulled a shining gold NBA championship ring off his finger, one of the three he'd earned. "I never got one of these in college, boys, and I'd sure like to." Excited whispering started up again.

As he reached into his right pocket I couldn't help staring at his ring. He removed a sheet of paper. "Coach Collier was kind enough to jot down a starting lineup he'd drawn up for this season." I looked over at Josh, a sense of relief surfacing on both our faces. We'd be starting after all. Lamar looked over the paper for a few seconds. "I respect Coach Collier very much, but today we start from scratch." He crumpled the sheet into a ball and threw the paper toward the sideline. "We'll find a lineup that works. For now, you can start running. I'll tell you when to stop. And if you finish last on my court, you clean up after practice."

Before we ran, Leroy had to speak. He never went quietly. "Coach, this isn't fair, I'll always finish last. Look at me,

I'm twice as big as these guys." We all laughed. The big man had a point.

"Leave the excuses at the door, Leroy." Coach blew his whistle. "Go!"

We ran silently for at least an hour. I was deep in thought, knowing that the sheet Coach Williams crumpled up had my name penciled in as the starting point guard. We trudged around the baseline, covered from head to toe in sweat. Some guys could barely move, feet dragging past Coach, who taunted us. "Not in the shape you thought you were, huh? Keep running. One more lap with heart, then you can go home." He made his way to a comfortable seat in the stands.

Leroy Hill finished dead last after exerting all he had to stay with the pack. Exhausted, he began to pick up the balls and place them into bins at center court. The rest of the guys walked toward the locker room, whispering about Coach Williams and his ridiculous practice. One by one, we turned our heads toward Leroy. We stopped moving toward the comfort of a hot shower to help our teammate. Grabbing towels and dropping to the floor, we cleaned the court together. A sense of unity had been established. Succeed together, fail together, run together, clean together. I looked to the corner of the bleachers as I erased pools of sweat with my towel. Coach sat there, smiling. This was what he'd had in mind all along.

The first game of my sophomore season was against Lincoln College. The night before we left on a two day trip to Savannah, Georgia, I went to the gym to rid myself of any last minute jitters. After thirty minutes of putrid shooting, I worried that my jump shot wouldn't be making the road trip. "Release, follow through." My words bounced off the walls in the empty gymnasium.

A voice startled me from behind. "Your elbow's popping out on every shot you miss." Coach Williams approached me.

I tucked my elbow close to my ribs. "All right." I spoke as I shot a few more. "Elbow tucked, release and follow through." I made three in a row.

Coach smiled, "Fundamentals, Tony. That's all this game is."

I cradled the ball under my arm and faced him, "Coach Williams? It's no big deal but — do you remember me? Do you remember meeting Mike and me?" I'd been meaning to ask him this question since the moment he took over the team.

Coach put his arm around me. "I remember you both. What happened to your brother was a tragedy. He was a great player." He forced a smile. "I guess you made your way back onto that high school team after all. Picked up that state title too. Pretty impressive comeback, Hope."

I couldn't believe he remembered me. "I never had a chance to thank you for that." Coach Williams must have heard this all the time. He knew the effect his words had. People really listen to professional athletes. I know I did.

Coach grabbed the basketball from me, palming the leather by his side. "I need you to step up and be a leader this year, Tony." He started dribbling. The ball moved so swiftly between his hands, I thought he had the thing programmed. "In high school, you and your brother thought you two were the best players in the world. That confidence made you better. Every great player needs that swagger. I want to see it this year. That's how you'll lead this team."

I knew exactly what Coach was talking about. Back in high school, I used to glide up the floor, ease in my step. I dared defenders to guard me. That confidence vanished the night Mike was shot. "I miss playing with him, Coach. I miss him so much out there."

Coach responded, "Tony, I can help you take your gift all the way. That'll be the best thing you could ever do for your brother. All you need to do is believe in yourself." He pulled a jump shot that bricked off the back heel of the rim. "And remember to keep that elbow tucked." His smile matched mine. "You better get some sleep tonight. Bus leaves at six-thirty in the morning."

When we crossed into Georgia two days later, the sound of tires clearing paths through muddy roads disrupted the silence. Hours passed without a word spoken. Seats were filled with listless bodies, whose nervous looks and dazed expressions spoke volumes about the pressures of the upcoming season. First games are like first dates, you have no idea what's going to happen.

An hour outside of Savannah, Coach Williams instructed our bus driver to pull over. He stood in front of the team with an angry expression. "Are we a bunch of mimes or are we a basketball team? No one's said a word in here since North Carolina. Did you guys forget how to talk to one another? Everybody get off!" The bus stopped and the noise from the tires ceased.

We stepped out, expecting the verbal lashing to continue. Our collective posture resembled a unit in the army. We awaited the wrath of our sergeant. Instead, we each received an empty fruit basket. Lamar's expression softened. "Pick yourself out a nice peach." Coach grabbed one from a pile. "We're in Georgia now, best peaches in the world." He took a bite and the guys stared at one another, wondering if Coach had lost his mind. Our shoulders dropped and we walked around the small fruit stand in who knows where, Georgia, surveying the scenery. Everyone was talking now. Big country bugs flew by our heads and hanging trees blew in a strong breeze. A farmer named Tyler took us on a short walk to the peach trees. I'd never climbed a tree before, so I asked Farmer Gibby to pick mine.

We all jumped back onto the bus, each gripping a fresh Georgia peach. As I sat in my seat and took a bite, I realized what Lamar had done. He'd taken our minds off basketball. I listened to comments around the bus, "These things sure are juicy." C.J. Katz finished his peach in about three bites.

Leroy Hill spoke with a full mouth. "Yeah, they drip right down your chin. "

Josh tapped me on the shoulder. "You ever had a peach like this, Tony?"

I took a bite and stared at Coach. "No peach trees in Harlem."

Coach Williams agreed. "That's the truth."

When we arrived at Lincoln College for our first game of the season, peach juice stuck to our fingers. Our first assignment was to clean our hands. Then we'd worry about Lincoln.

We were loose when game time arrived. The whistle blew and big Leroy Hill tapped the ball back to me, the starting point guard. I reminded myself of the game plan, "Play with swagger. Penetrate. Attack the defense. Bring it." On the first possession, I stormed through defenders and brought it to the rim with a two handed dunk. Rattled, Lincoln missed their first couple of shots, then a couple more. They never fully recovered from our 16-2 onslaught to open the game.

I finished with twenty points in a decisive win that secured Coach Williams's first victory, and catapulted our national ranking from sixteen to eleven. That recognition brought along large expectations. We met the challenge, surviving our first eighteen games without a blemish. As our season turned down the home stretch, dreams of perfection kept me awake at night. I looked at our schedule. January 21st, at Trenton, a game I'd circled in red. This was the last roadblock between us and a perfect record.

We entered Trenton State's Kennel for the second straight year. Within five minutes, we'd jumped out to a seven point lead. I dribbled up the floor, turning my head as Gibby hooted for the ball. After zipping him a pass, I hustled back to play defense. I didn't think there would be a rebound. Seeing him set to shoot usually meant two points.

Only this time, when Josh released his jumper, Larry "The Monster" Murphy extended his yardstick arm and deflected the ball. Murphy grabbed the rock and began dribbling clumsily on the fast break. I blocked his lane to the hoop, the last line of defense. Murphy came charging at me like a bull searching for red. Only I didn't get out of his way. I held ground, trying to draw an offensive foul. Larry wasn't agile enough to avoid the collision and he probably didn't want to. The star linebacker for Trenton's football team loved a good hit. I closed my eyes, ready for the train wreck. His shoulder blasted me backward and my ribs smacked the hardwood. Our awkward crash landing buried my twisted ankle beneath his massive body.

The official blew his whistle. "Blocking foul, fourteen defense." You'd think seeing me flattened would've earned a little compassion from the referee. No such luck.

I tried to stand, but crumbled to the floor. My leg couldn't support me. A throbbing pain crawled up my ankle, which was inflating like a balloon. "I'm okay," I said, grabbing Josh's arm for support. Trying to stand again, I failed, dropping in agony.

Coach Williams and a few of the guys carried me to the sidelines. I was helped through long hallways beneath The Kennel. A door opened to the outside and I was led into the back of an ambulance. To add insult to injury, we lost that game to Trenton by six.

At the emergency room, X-rays revealed that my ankle had broken in two places. I would miss the championship tournament.

CHAPTER ELEVEN

WIN-OR-GO-HOME

My broken ankle ended my sophomore season. All I could do was watch in pain as Montana University thumped us in the opening round of the championship tournament. Two years of college had passed. All I had to show for my efforts was one season on the bench, and another nursing a broken ankle — hardly a storybook career.

That summer I limped home to Harlem with a cast plastered to my leg. When the doctor finally cut the thing off, my shrunken twig needed rehabilitation. Each morning I would get up early. Not to go to the courts like the old days, but to join Mike at Harlem Memorial Hospital for our workouts. He had spent the past twenty-five months rehabbing there.

While I did strengthening exercises on my snapped ankle, Mike attacked bigger problems. His mornings consisted of massage and electro-therapy. Nurses would hook Mike up to an electric stimulation machine, hoping to awaken his sleeping muscles. He did this for hours, never missing a day. A lot of people gave up after the doctors delivered the long odds of recovery from paralysis. Mike just tried harder.

On the last day of my rehab I watched Mike go through his electro-therapy. Two nurses attached strange wires to his legs. He looked at me and shot a thumbs up, convincing me to believe the same way he did. The nurse turned the machine on and immediately Mike's right leg flinched. I thought I'd imagined it.

"I felt my leg, T!" I hadn't imagined anything. Mike turned to face his nurse, "Did you see that, Bertha?" He asked proudly.

Bertha clapped her hands and gasped. "I saw it, Mike. Your leg moved." She recorded something on her chart.

"Well, what are you waiting for, shock me again!" They did. Again and again. His leg had flinched for the first time in twenty-five months that morning and we waited all day for the second. But there was no more movement. Finally, we left the hospital. Mike was no longer smiling. He was intense, looking at me the way he used to on the basketball court. "I'll move again, T. These legs are gonna wake up."

Mike sat at home for the rest of the day, staring at his right leg. Waiting for it to move again, wondering how it moved in the first place. When he hit his pillow that night, all he could do was cross his fingers and hope that his flinch was the first move, and not the last.

After six weeks of Mom's home cooking, my time in Harlem was up. I hopped on a graffiti-bathed number Six, the hottest train on the tracks in August. When I stepped off an hour later, I was a block from the apartment I would be sharing with Josh. Gibby had become one of my closest friends. Just thinking about the stories he would tell quickened my step to the apartment. Like the time he set up three cows on the court in his backyard and dribbled in between and around them like they were defenders. Or the time he lost a bet with a friend and had to dye his hair blue for a month.

I huffed and puffed up eight flights of steep stairs, lugging my green duffle bag all the way. When I arrived at our front door, I threw the thing to the ground and pounded with my right fist. "Hey Farmer!" The temperature hovered near one hundred degrees, likening the stairwell to a sauna. A sweat river dripped down from my forehead. "Open up, Gibby, I'm melting out here."

I guessed our apartment wasn't equipped with air conditioning either, because when the door opened, Josh stood shirtless. I did a double take before slapping his hand and greeting him. Gibby looked like he'd been eating too much hay. He was huge! "What happened?" I asked jokingly, "Did you eat Josh?"

He was at least twenty-five pounds heavier than the nineteen-year-old toothpick who left campus six weeks earlier. "Are you kidding me, Farmer? What are they putting in the corn out there?" I started laughing as he grabbed my duffle and flung it into my room like a paperweight. My two closest friends, Mike and Josh, had both turned into bodybuilders.

"Welcome back, Hope." Josh flexed his muscles, "Done with the bones jokes now?"

I pushed him backward laughing, "You've still got

bones, Farmer."

Three months after moving in, our junior season started. The task at hand was straightforward — win the national championship. That journey began with what should have been a workout against Memphis State University. Yet routine turned difficult when Josh and I opened the game by shooting a combined 2 for 14 from the field. Four minutes in, we trailed by eleven to a grossly inferior team.

As the point guard, my job was to calm the tempo and exude confidence. Although my shooting touch was off, I could still toy with the defense. Two defenders drew close. Their waving arms resembled the motions of people frantically flagging down a taxi. Calmly, I swirled the ball around my back to avoid the swiping hands. Seconds later I fired a chest pass to my wing. I waited for Josh to bury the open jumper. He stood motionless, confidence shattered after his dismal one-for-eight start. The shot clock ticked down to two when he threw the ball back to me. I was forced to shoot off balance and my consequent air-ball left me embarrassed and aggravated.

On the next play we suffered a complete defensive lapse. Memphis State scored uncontested, extending their lead to thirteen. Coach Williams signaled for a timeout.

I came to the bench in a rage. "Take the shot if you're open, Gibson! That's why you're the *shoot*ing guard, you shoot!" I took a sip from a water bottle and threw it to the floor in frustration.

Josh's face turned tomato red. "How about you stop showboating up the floor? Around the back, between the legs — this isn't the Tony Hope Show!"

Coach Williams stepped between us. "Enough! Enough of this finger pointing! Both of you get comfortable on the bench. Hooper, Jackson, get in there." Coach kicked the scorer's table, more upset than I'd ever seen him. "You two better start acting like captains, not crybabies. How are we gonna succeed if our stars are whining like four-year-olds?"

I retreated quietly to the end of the bench. The next hour and a half was torture. Josh and I sat beside one another silently as our abandoned teammates chased Memphis State up and down the floor. I would look over at Gibby, he'd glance back, but neither one of us would budge. So we sat on the bench in stubborn silence, refusing to apologize.

After the defeat, we boarded an airplane for a three hour flight to New York. I sat in a window seat, the aisle separating Josh and me. Before the plane took off Coach Williams stood in front of the guys. "That was a terrible loss. You can thank your captains for putting themselves before the team." No one dared speak a word. "We have to make a choice, right here and now. Are we going to succeed together, or fail as individuals?"

I sat with my head leaning against the window. Coach's speech had me thinking. A moment later I felt a tapping on my shoulder. "Tony." I heard Josh's muffled voice through the sounds of the takeoff.

I looked his way. "Listen Gibby, I - "

Josh cut me off. "Let's squash it, T. Besides, you were right, I should have taken the shot."

"I was the jerk. I should never have called you out like that in front of the team." I extended my hand to Josh. "His-

113

tory, right?"

"Of course," he grabbed my hand and shook. "I know you just want to win. But we can't win this thing without you and me being on the same page. This is *our* team. " He paused. "And this year may be our last shot. Leroy's graduating. And you know we can't win this thing without him. Plus — " He stopped. "Who knows? You could be leaving too." I didn't respond. The team didn't need any further distractions. But Josh was right, if everything went as planned, my junior year *would* be my last. I would forego my senior season for the NBA.

Finally, I spoke, tiptoeing around my future plans. "Well, this is our year then."

Our rocky start didn't hinder a great regular season. We were winners in twenty-seven of thirty games, pulling out victory in each of our last seventeen. The whining ceased, and Josh and I played in perfect rhythm.

We entered the tournament as the number one ranked team in the country for the first time in UNY's history. Hoffman Arena in Chicago was where our journey began. A bullseye had been placed on our back. Every team would be gunning for us.

The excitement of a win or go home contest is the reason the championship tournament is the greatest event in sports. Our first round game pitted us against Cheyenne College, a small religious school in South Dakota. For the first time in three years, I would be part of the playoffs.

Little Cheyenne College knew what was at stake. The

soldiers from South Dakota wore their game faces during warm-ups. But a few moments later, when Leroy Hill stepped onto the court, their jaws dropped. The Wheateaters would need stepping stools to defend the six-foot-eleven beast. He was eight inches taller than anyone on their team.

The game began with a 20-0 burst. We simply fed the ball into Leroy, who dunked over defenders on virtually every possession. Cheyenne's Coach, Bobby Alvarez, signaled for timeout after timeout. But neither he, nor his under talented troops, could temper the massacre. Final score — Lightning Storm, 88 Wheateaters, 46.

Getting that win under my belt eased almost three years of anxiety. But our goal wasn't to win a single game. By the time Cedar Hills College took the floor as our second opponent, Cheyenne's destruction was a faded memory. Victory here would propel us into the round of sixteen. Once again, defeat would send us home.

I played the game of my life against Cedar Hills, scoring a career high 42 points. We pounded the Coyotes by seventeen. The shooting clinic fueled my confidence tank to full as I stepped onto a plane bound for Dallas and the round of sixteen.

My mental picture of Texas was completely different than reality. Aside from a few country music bars and an occasional cowboy, I'd say the Wild West was pretty mild. Although Pennsylvania farm country was a few thousand miles northeast, Gibby made himself feel right at home. Five minutes after we'd stepped off the plane, he was halfway through a bowl of Texas chili, and his head was covered by a huge cowboy hat. He'd tip the thing awkwardly to every girl we passed and refused to remove it from his head until we stepped onto the court for warm-ups, three days later.

In our game against Oklahoma Tech, Josh was money. But Ian Epstein, Tech's five-foot-nine sharpshooter, stepped up to the challenge. Josh and Ian traded baskets like baseball cards. And little Epstein was almost a hero that day. That is, until his jumper clanked off the rim in the closing seconds. Leroy Hill grabbed the board to complete our narrow escape. Just one victory separated us from the Last Four, college basketball's grandest stage.

First we'd have to put a stop to San Diego University's fairytale run. After pulling upsets against Northwest Tennessee, Southern Florida, and the Howling Wolves from Boulder College, they faced us in the round of eight. We pummeled the "sunshine boys" by twenty that day.

Next stop: Los Angeles, the sight of the Last Four.

We arrived the following morning. Josh, Leroy, and I spent the day sightseeing. I took a picture next to the HOLLYWOOD sign and Gibby bought another stupid hat. Meanwhile, Leroy was sucking down California ice cream like water, the guy had four strawberry cones before we stopped for lunch! There was nothing anyone could do to wipe the grins from our faces.

Until game day, that is, when we trailed Upper Nevada with seven minutes remaining. After fouling out of the contest I tried to rally my teammates. I couldn't sit there helplessly and witness a third straight season end from the bench, so I swung a towel in circles above my head, believing the guys would come through.

When Leroy Hill was slapped in the face by the swinging arm of Upper Nevada's Humphrey Sloan, the game turned. The happiest, and biggest guy on the floor had become enraged. This was bad news for Sloan. Josh began feeding our center in the post on nearly every possession. Though it wasn't strawberry ice cream, Leroy was eating everything up inside. His twelve points in the final six minutes catapulted us to a dramatic victory. Gibby was right, we couldn't win without our big guy.

That come from behind win set up an intriguing tilt for the title, the University of New York against Virginia State College. For me, this wasn't just any match-up. The Colonials were led by a pair of familiar faces — Brooklyn's Backcourt. My bitter high school rivals, James Thomas and Walter Randolph, had guided their college team to the title game as well. Although the match-up could no longer be billed as "Brooklyn's Backcourt vs. The Hope Brothers," basketball fans everywhere pulled their seats up a little closer as a heated high school rivalry was renewed.

The game would be played at the Los Angeles Basketball Center, in front of a sellout crowd of 26,000 fans, not to mention the fifty-million viewers who would be watching from their living room couches. Josh and I were interviewed quite a bit on game day. I repeated rehearsed lines Coach had taught us. He insisted the key to success with the media was to never be original. I obliged, delivering corny line after corny line.

When we left the interview room and made our way onto the court for warm-ups, a voice called out from the other end of the floor. "Hey Hope, don't get too stuck on yourself. You're gonna get beat down tonight. Mike isn't here to bail you out this time." I didn't even have to look. James Thomas, the point guard I hadn't seen in five years, was *still* talking.

Just before tip-off, Thomas continued his chatter, this time targeting Gibby, "You're not in Pennsylvania anymore, Gibson. You've never seen moves like this, country boy. I'm gonna light you up."

We controlled the tip. Josh took two dribbles and swished a three-pointer. He approached Thomas. "Light *who* up?" The country boy could hang with anyone, both with his words and his jumpers. He hit his first four shots and did something that even Mike failed to do. He shut James Thomas up. VSC called a timeout trailing 10 – 4. Josh pointed at Thomas as he made his way to the huddle. Thomas looked away and I could barely contain my laughter.

When we came back onto the floor, the Colonials double-teamed Gibby. Silencing him had become their main objective. I took this as a personal challenge and began attacking. I nailed a few jump shots, made a reverse lay-up, and drew a couple of fouls on Walter Randolph. Our lead had stretched to 30-17 when VSC called for time.

On the ensuing inbound, Thomas fired a laser into Randolph's chest. Walter turned to face me, confidently palming the ball with his right hand. I reached out and poked the leather from his grip. Josh anticipated the fast break and bolted toward the other end. Thomas gave chase as I launched a pass. Josh gracefully caught the rock over his shoulder like Jerry Rice, and leaped toward a dunk. Thomas rose alongside. Realizing he couldn't block Gibby's shot, he grabbed him by the shoulder. With all his might, he violently spun him in mid-air. Josh's huge frame tumbled to the ground. The popping sound of bone smashing against wood left every face in the arena cringing.

I ran over and helped Josh to his feet. Meanwhile, Thomas pleaded his case to the referee. "He's all right. I was just going for the ball." Despite his campaigning, the ref issued Thomas a technical foul.

Coach Williams tried to substitute Tracy Hooper for an injured Gibby. But Josh refused to leave the floor, waving Hooper back to the sidelines. His right arm hung lifeless, yet he stubbornly pushed forward. He walked slowly to the free throw line, cradling the ball in his working arm. Amazingly, he made one of his two foul shots with his left hand.

Although Josh's heroics were well noted, he wasn't the same player for the rest of that half. He couldn't shoot, which meant Thomas and Randolph both shadowed me. Our eleven point advantage quickly transformed into a five point deficit. During halftime, Josh was taken to the emergency room.

With Gibby in the hospital, I had to find new ways to lead the team. Throughout my life, I'd been feeding the ball to my wing. For twenty-one years, I was the second option. But as I stepped out of the locker room for the final twenty minutes of the season, something strange happened. Everything became quiet. My usual thoughts about the game ceased. The sounds of my breathing were audible. I could almost hear myself blink. When I picked up a basketball, I swished a jump shot effortlessly. What was that? I thought. My fingers and toes began tingling. A moment of trepidation was replaced by a picture of Mike in the hospital bed after his accident, "Someday you're going to have a moment where everything will get clear…" A wave of joy rushed through my body. My moment had arrived. "You've always been a great player, always." His voice echoed in my head. I threw up three more jumpers, stepping back a few feet with every shot. Swish, swish, nothing but net.

I assume Thomas continued his trash talking during that second half, but I don't really remember. My mind had entered a foreign land, a place all athletes dream of visiting. Yes, something strange was definitely happening. I had entered the Zone. All the great ones speak about their trips to this land, a world where the difficult becomes routine, where defenders have no chance, and where all noise is muted. The moment of clarity that Mike predicted had come to pass.

Virginia State defenders started moving in slow motion, and in a matter of moments, where they moved was irrelevant. I'd become unstoppable. Nearly every shot I took swished through the net perfectly. During the final twenty minutes of that game, I attempted seventeen shots and made all but two. My thirty-three second half points smashed a playoff record, and led UNY to our first Championship in school history.

When you see me today, look at my hand. If I'm not on the court playing, I'm always wearing my ring, forever reminded of my teammates, our dream season, and the place I went that night.

CHAPTER TWELVE

JUMPING SHIP

When our bus pulled up to campus, 10,000 students were holding banners, throwing confetti, and singing the UNY fight song. We were national champions and everyone was suddenly a basketball fan.

We made our way through the boisterous crowd, toward our locker room. Josh threw some of his souvenir hats to the screaming fans. A pretty girl with straight black hair caught his cowboy hat. She placed it on her head and winked at Josh, who raised his arms high in triumph. He pointed at her coolly and then tripped on his way into the locker room. Another slick move by Gibby.

When I emptied my locker for the off season I knew my last moments as a student-athlete had arrived. After winning the championship, I decided to skip my senior year at UNY. I would declare myself eligible for the NBA draft. But I wasn't stupid. I knew that basketball wouldn't last forever. My business degree was as valuable as my jump shot any day. By taking summer school classes, I would still earn my diploma.

I started my off season workout two days after returning from Los Angeles. When I arrived at the gym, I lugged a large rack of balls from the equipment room. I practiced until my shoes were tired and my throat was dry. When I made my way to the drinking fountain, I heard the distinct footsteps of Coach Williams from the other end of the court. Though I couldn't make out his face, the loud snapping of his sandals made his presence certain. Aside from formal gatherings and games, Coach was always in flip-flops. Blisters and bruises felt better in a pair of sandals. Nobody knew this better than the man who owned the most famous pair of feet in the world.

I started to panic as he approached. I'd been avoiding this confrontation for the past two days. Disappointing my hero wasn't something I looked forward to. How was I going to tell him that I wasn't coming back? What would I say? How could I choose the NBA over another year in his program?

Coach Willliams spoke over his clicking sandals. "Hey Tony." I motioned hello, my mouth too dry to speak. "Real impressed that you're back in here two days after. A lot of guys win one and get complacent. You're hungry for another one, though. I like that." I felt even worse about the news I was about to deliver. I leaned in to get a sip of water, game planning what I was about to say.

I wiped the water from my lips with the bottom of my shirt. "I wanted to get a head start on next year, I mean - " The time had come. I couldn't skirt around the truth any longer. "Coach?"

"What's up?" he asked as he grabbed a ball and spun it on his pointer finger.

I swallowed loudly. "I wanted to talk to you about next season. I think…" I paused. "I'm going to the NBA." Coach took a shot that barely caught the rim. I'd never seen him miss the basket by that much.

He shook his head. "Well, that certainly wasn't what I thought you were going to say. But if that's your choice - " His voice faded as he glared at me sternly. I averted his eyes. The silence grew heavy.

I broke the quiet, "I'm sorry, Coach."

"You're ready to play in the NBA next year, huh?" Coach asked with his hand on my shoulder.

"Sure I'm ready." I spoke with confidence.

There was a long pause. Coach waited to speak, formulating something in his head. "Okay. Then you shouldn't have any problem beating a forty-one-year-old with creaky knees, right?" He cracked his knuckles loudly.

"What?" I asked, not believing the challenge Coach had put on the table.

"You heard me." He retorted.

"C'mon Coach, you don't really think you can run with me, do you?" I didn't want to beat up on my hero in his old age. The guy standing across from me was a gray haired replica of the ballplayer he once was.

Coach took offense. A competitive grumble became audible in his voice. "We'll play to eleven. If you win, you have my blessings; you *are* ready. But if you lose, if I beat you, then you show up to practice next season." Coach was serious, extending his hand to seal the deal. "What do you say?"

I could have walked away and told him my decision was final. I could have headed right out the door to the NBA. But how do you turn your back on your hero? I grabbed his hand and shook. "You've got a deal."

He emerged from the locker room a few minutes later, wearing high tops and an old New York Pride jersey. He stood at the top of the key. "Check it up."

"Don't you need to stretch those old muscles?" I cracked a smile.

Coach stepped up. "Shut up, Hope. I'm ready." He pushed the ball into my chest. The look in his eyes had a focus that I had never seen before. His easy smile had been replaced by a frightening competitive glare. Right then, I realized something — this wasn't Coach Williams anymore. I'd awoken "Sweet Feet."

I checked the ball up and dug in defensively. Coach continued to stare me down. I directed my eyes toward his hips, in anticipation of his first move. He took two long, slow dribbles with his right hand. Then I saw his hips shift left. He was trying to cross me up. My feet shuffled quickly and I extended my right hand for the swipe. But I never felt the ball. "Sweet Feet" danced past me, exploding toward a wide open lay-up. Instead of dropping in a finger roll, he stopped beneath the basket, then dribbled back to the top of the key. "That was a free lesson, the next one's gonna cost you a bucket."

I had never seen a crossover that fast in my life. "Sweet Feet" continued talking, "Didn't think the old man would tie you in knots, did you?" He faked to his left quickly and I flinched, obviously rattled. Coach just laughed. "Here I go, son."

He dribbled right at me. As I prepared my body for the contact, Coach stopped on a dime. He quickly slid the ball behind his back and nailed a jumper. "One-nothing college hoops." He was taunting me with the promise I'd made to return to school if he beat me. "This is just a taste of what an NBA point guard can do to you. You still ready? You still jumping ship?"

I nodded, settling in on defense. Coach dribbled like the ball was an extension of his hand, behind his back, through his legs, through my legs. All the while I swiped and swatted, but never once did I touch leather. I remembered being a kid, watching "Sweet Feet" make worthy opponents look silly. Fumbling and tripping, I knew I had become one of them.

Much of the game continued in the same manner, with "Sweet Feet" scoring at will, and me standing defenseless. He swished pull-up jumpers, made fancy lay-ups, and his old legs even rose for a slam. Meanwhile, I barely got a shot off. Before I knew what had happened — "Ten-two," Coach called out. "Game point, Hope."

I crept up next to him, his back to my chest. He talked to me as he dribbled, "One more year Hope, then you'll be ready."

I swiped and missed, sweat dripping from everywhere. "I'm ready now, old man."

He faked to his left. I slipped and nearly fell.

"You need another year, Hope. I believe in you, son. If you stay this last year, you'll be a better ballplayer." I swiped at the ball again and missed, "a smarter ballplayer," again I swiped and missed, "and a better person." With his comment, Coach faded back and shot a high archer. The ball danced on the rim and dropped through. "Game over, son."

I stood quietly and waited for "Sweet Feet" to say something else. Coach patted me on the shoulder and handed me the basketball. He turned his back and walked toward the locker room. The gym was silent. All I heard were his squeaking sneakers marching in a victory parade across the court.

Just as he was about to enter through the double doors to the locker room, he turned and faced me. "Summer practice starts in three weeks, Hope. I'll see you there."

I had given Coach my word. And on the first day of practice he did see me there. While a part of me was still peering at the NBA draft, wondering when I would have been selected, the other part of me knew my game still needed some fine-tuning. "Sweet Feet," three years removed from the game, had humiliated me. If I was going to take the torch as Harlem's greatest player, I needed to continue learning from the man who currently held that honor.

I averaged career highs in points and assists during my senior season. And once again, we entered the tournament as a favorite to win. But much like my sophomore year, we got ahead of ourselves. After running off three straight victories and advancing to the round of eight, we fell asleep against the Durham Dukes. They sent us packing, me for good.

Two months after the season ended, the UNY gymnasium filled up again. This time for graduation. Being in that gym and wearing a gown in place of my jersey brought a dif-

126

ferent sort of satisfaction. I stood in an endless line, waiting for my name to be called. People weren't watching my every move, cheering for me to dunk or throw an alley-oop.

When I stepped up to the podium, Dean Watters handed me a scrolled piece of paper that I held high. Mom started crying. No one in our family had ever graduated college. Mine was the first diploma inscribed with the name Hope. Two weeks later, Mike was on the podium in Harlem, earning our family's second degree.

CHAPTER THIRTEEN

HARLEM'S HOPE

I made my way back to Harlem with a college degree in hand. After six weeks of waiting, I nearly slept through draft day. I woke up around noon, threw on a pair of old shorts, and ran three miles, stopping at Mario's Pizza Shop for lunch. Mario, a short balding man of about fifty, recognized me immediately. He shook my hand and slid me a slice of pizza. "Here you go, Tony. Extra pepperoni, just like you like it." He dropped the morning paper on the counter. "You read this yet?" His thick Italian accent rang through with every word.

I shook my head, "No, anything good?"

"Check out the back page, I think you'll like it." I turned the paper over. A glaring headline caught my eye, "Pride Trade Gentry, *Hoping* for UNY Standout." The article confirmed that the New York Pride had traded Lionel Gentry to Florida for the number one pick in the draft. A smile cracked from the corner of my face as I looked up at Mario. His eyebrows raised just below his balding head. "Harlem's Hope playing for the Pride. Not much better than that." He shaped a pile of dough in his hands. "And after you get picked, Tony, don't forget us."

"I won't forget. See you tomorrow, Mario." I threw him a couple of bucks and left.

With the draft drawing closer, I retreated to the Jungle. Although I'd been invited to attend the draft in Miami, I wasn't going. The day before Mike had undergone emergency surgery to repair his left wrist. He'd shattered it during rehab. I put my suntan lotion back in my drawer. Our family trip to Florida had been cancelled.

I wanted to watch the draft with Mike, but my brother insisted that I shouldn't spend my big day in a musty hospital room. So I called up Gibby and told him to come to the Jungle. He, too, was eligible for the draft, but wasn't projected as a first-round pick. Miami Arena's cushy red chairs were reserved for these first-rounders. Without a seat, Josh would spend his day in Harlem. Good news or bad, it would eventually find us at the Jungle.

When I showed up at the courts, a group of guys were gathered around Gibby. They laughed hysterically as he waved his arms in the air, elaborating on the details of another tall tale. I joined the circle. Nobody told stories quite like Josh. Once I heard him talking about cows again, I moved away and began shooting.

I looked around at the faces pinned against the fence. I watched them watching me. In forty minutes, the number-one pick in the draft would be announced. I surveyed the scene. Beyond the fence, a laundromat with a brick face and opened doors began attracting a large crowd. The television was on, and as people passed by, they stopped in. In the street, two kids pedaling scooters pointed at me. A middle-aged woman waved a sign from her balcony. **"MAKE US PROUD, TONY."** Four older men sat out front playing checkers in worn out lawn chairs, unaffected by the hoopla. Young kids squirted each other with water guns. Honking cars drove by, music blasted, and the smells of summer hung in the air.

My focus shifted back to the court. We split up teams and a pick up game broke out. I was dribbling at the top of the key when a young defender tried to snake the ball away from me. The kid was overanxious, obviously trying to show me what he could do. I remembered when I was his age, constantly trying to prove to the older guys that I belonged. He was swatting at the ball the same way I used to. Time to be the teacher, I thought. I crossed over from my right to my left a few times, teasing the youngster. He'd creep closer, and I'd pull the ball back, waiting for the moment he leaned the wrong way. When he made his false move, I'd dart past. After a few easy lay-ups, Josh switched to defend me. I looked over at the kid who wore disappointment all over his face. The ball hopped out of bounds and I had a moment to speak with him. "Keep your eye on the hips, not the ball. Don't just swat. Have patience. And never let'em see you're frustrated!"

These were the same lessons Lamar had taught me. Generations of playmakers passed down knowledge on these courts. I was now one of them. And who knows, maybe that kid would grow up to be Harlem's next hope.

Seconds later, I heard some commotion at the

laundromat. "They're about to pick!" I took a jump shot over the top of Josh, pretending not to feel the excitement. Pretending not to wonder about the New York Pride and their number one pick. My shot wasn't close, smacking the front of the rim and bouncing back into my hands. I was curious as to what was happening across the street. But our game was tied at ten — next basket wins. I eyed the laundromat for a moment, then held the ball in front of Josh. I picked up my dribble and pump faked. He bit hard, leaving his feet. I dropped a soft twelve-footer through the net. Game over.

Trying to remain calm, I sat on a rusted bench adjacent to the courts. I whispered to myself, "Have they picked yet?" My answer came quickly as the noise from the laundromat grew frantic. I turned in my seat, positioning my body to get a better view. The small television set was out of my range. A moment later, a pack of kids ran toward me. The smallest in the bunch sprinted onto the court shouting, "The Pride picked Tony Hope! They got Harlem's Hope!"

With that, the whole place erupted.

Josh was the first to run over to me. His powerful hug nearly broke my ribs. "Number one pick!" He lifted me in the air. "Now aren't you glad I blocked that closet door?"

I didn't know what to say. Without Josh, none of this would have happened. "You're the man, Gibby. Thanks." Josh started to walk away as people gathered all around me. In between shaking a hundred hands, I shouted out, "Hey Gibson!" He turned back. I yelled over the crowd, "I don't care if you are a farmer. You and I are brothers." With that, I realized where I needed to be. A few miles away in a hospital bed, my

132

twin brother was recovering from surgery on his wrist. Alone, he was watching all of our dreams come true. I had to share the moment with him. I invited Gibby to come with me, but he wanted to stay put until the television called out his name.

I sat back down on the bench and untied my shoelaces, a huge smile painted across my face. I put on the sandals "Sweet Feet" had given me as a graduation present. Slipping them on made me think of my mentor. My life had been patterned after his: from the Park, down the street to the Jungle, to Harlem's PS-44, through four years at the University of New York, and now, as the point guard for the New York Pride. I stood up from the bench, sandals snapping loudly the way his did. Reaching down to pick up my high-tops, I only came up with a handful of air. In the chaos, I'd placed my sneakers right beside me. Now they were gone. I checked under the bench, behind the bench, and on the bench. Had someone stolen my shoes? I looked around the crowded courts to see who had taken them. After some searching, I gave up. I had to see my brother.

When I walked toward the exit, hordes of people began lining the fence. As I passed by my neighbors, the metal links shook wildly. A chant began, "Hope!...Hope!... Hope!" Bouncing balls ceased as the chanting grew louder, "Hope!...Hope!...Hope!"

A little girl tapped me on the shoulder and pointed toward the sky. I glanced up. Two guys were boosting a kid up the fence. He was holding my sneakers while tying the shoelaces together around the highest part. My sneakers hung the way "Sweet Feet's" did. Like Harlem's flag. As I walked away, the lingering chant followed me for close to three blocks.

133

I spent the rest of that afternoon celebrating with Mike and Mom in the hospital. We watched as Gibby was selected thirty-third by Dallas. Now he could buy himself a new cowboy hat and wear it fulltime. As for me, my wardrobe wouldn't change a bit. Towers Memorial Arena was only ten minutes from our apartment in Harlem.

Four months later, on the morning of my first NBA game, I sat in our living room. The same living room I had grown up in. Only now the tired walls were refreshed by a fresh coat of paint, my reflection mirrored off a big screen television, and I sat on a leather couch big enough for Shaquille O'Neal. Even the front door was brand new. I was tired of picking off those paint chips.

I heard the humming of Mike's new electric wheelchair behind me. "What's up, Mike?"

He pulled his chair parallel to the couch. "Not much."

"Game day today." I smiled.

Mike spoke quietly. "Yeah, I know. I'm excited, you?"

"Excited, nervous, everything." There was an uncomfortable silence. "I want you to be there tonight, Mike. I got you and Mom tickets."

He stared at the floor while he spoke, "You know I can't do that, Tony."

"Sure you can. I got you a seat in the corner, nobody's gonna see you."

"Nobody's gonna see me, is that what you said?" His voice rose, "You know that's not true. When I roll down that aisle, every camera in that place is gonna focus on me and this chair. They're gonna tell the story about that night again." His face dropped. I hadn't heard him mention the accident in over a year. "I don't want millions of people thinking 'poor Mike.' I want them thinking about you. This is your night. I'll watch the game from home."

I wanted to respond. I wanted my brother to be there. But I knew Mike, and I knew I wasn't going to win this battle. The silence in the room was replaced by the humming of his wheelchair as he left.

When I entered the Pride locker room no one was around. I flipped on the lights and walked into the center of the blue carpet where a huge Pride logo shone down from the ceiling. A clock on the wall read 3:30 p.m., four hours until game time. I moved in front of my locker and stared at my number 14 jersey, the name HOPE was printed in big blue letters across the back. I scanned the rest of the locker with wide eyes. I had six pairs of sneakers, size twelves, five pairs of practice shorts, a stack of t-shirts, headbands, wristbands and socks. I could dress a family of four with all this stuff.

One by one, my teammates began to filter into the locker room. After suiting up, we stepped onto the floor for warm-ups. I moved under the basket and began rebounding for veteran point guard Maurice Youngkin. Between his shots, I'd glance toward the corner of the front row. Empty seats stared back at me. Mom said she was coming. She should have been sitting there. I turned my attention back to the aging Youngkin. Watching him warm-up, I was sure I'd see time on the court that night. There was no way he could play a full forty-eight minutes.

I moved to the corner of the bench, a seat reserved for rookies. The ball tipped — still no sign of Mom. I didn't understand why she was late for my first NBA game. This wasn't like her at all. For the next ten minutes I looked like I was watching a tennis match. My head clicked back and forth between the game and the stands. Each time I glanced to the corner of the court, I expected to see Mom rushing through the aisle. My right leg shook, a nervous habit of mine.

When Coach Mark Clark noticed Youngkin pulling on his shorts, he signaled for time, fatigue setting in on his veteran. I moved into the huddle, glancing over Coach's shoulder at Mom's seat. Where could she possibly be? Suddenly I was frozen, petrified that something might have gone wrong with Mike's health. I searched my brain for some other reason that Mom would have been late to the game. All I could come up with was disaster.

"Hope!" I heard Coach Clark's husky voice, "Hope, you ready?"

I wasn't ready, but I had to be. I tore off my warm-ups. "I'm ready, Coach."

"You're in for Youngkin." He patted me on the back as I passed him and stepped onto the court.

I took one last look toward the stands. My mother was rushing to her seat in the same way I'd imagined. She'd made it after all. And just in time for my first moments in the NBA. Now I could focus on beating Chicago. I crouched down and touched the number forty-four on my sneakers, smiling at my mother, who was pointing up the aisle.

"What?" I mouthed, unsure of what she was doing. I

followed the path of her finger.

Behind her was the greatest sight of all.

Two security guards were clearing a path as Mike wheeled himself through crowds of people toward the front row. He'd been through hell, but he'd made it to my first game. Our eyes met as his chair came to a stop just beyond the out-of-bounds line. The security guards moved away from him, and Mike sat still, staring at me. And that's when something amazing happened.

My brother grabbed hold of both sides of his wheel-chair and the right side of his body began to shake violently. But the look on his face was serene as he fought and struggled to bring his legs back to life. I watched, mesmerized, as his right leg slowly crept into the air. A moment later, the left side of his body began to fight. And then a second leg inched into the air. This time faster and higher than the first. Slowly, he began to emerge from his chair. Using the strength in his arms, he pushed up from his seat until he was wobbling on his two stale legs. He stood quivering for a few long seconds. Mike Hope could move again! Mom grabbed him by the waist and guided him another step. I watched in silent awe as he plopped down, exhausted, into the front row seat.

His wheelchair sat beside him, vacated. Mike pointed to me from his seat, and we shared the look I'd always dreamed of. We'd made it. I was standing on an NBA court realizing our childhood dream. And Mike was on the sidelines, defying *all* the odds and *all* the doctors who told him he'd never walk again.

Dribbling up the floor was easy with Mike there with

me. I'd never felt so confident. I was an NBA player and I really belonged. In those moments the basket looked as big as an ocean, and I was the captain of a great ship with Mike as my first mate. I heard his voice as I passed the ball to an open teammate.

"I'm on your wing, T. On your wing if you need me."

TEST YOURSELF...ARE YOU A PROFESSIONAL READER?

Chapter 1: Fifteen Hours

Why was it that Terry Jackson could jump higher than Mike and Tony?

Why didn't Tony go with his brother to the party?

What does the title of this chapter, "Fifteen Hours," refer to?

ESSAY

Tony says that Mike had taken a "terrible shot" by leaving with Nick and Devon. What does he mean by this? Why didn't Tony want his brother hanging out with those guys?

Chapter 2: Shorty

Why did challenging Jason Helms to a game of one on one not seem like one of Tony's smarter ideas?

Describe Tony's defensive theory about staring at his opponents' hips.

At the end of the chapter, Tony says that he has "graduated." What does he mean by that?

ESSAY

Jason Helms got more than he bargained for during his game

against Tony. Tony gained respect despite his loss. Has there ever been a time in your life that you "lost but still won?" Explain.

Chapter 3: Locked Out

Why did Tony think that Mike had forgotten Mom?

What led Tony to falsely believe that he deserved special treatment when he showed up for high school tryouts?

What does the chapter's title, "Locked Out" refer to?

ESSAY

Coach Harris told Tony that "he had no respect for his elders." Was there a time in your life when you disrespected one of your elders, a coach, a teacher or a parent? What did you learn from this?

Chapter 4: Sweet Feet

Why was Tony surprised when Mike didn't look up at 'Sweet Feet's' window?

What occurred to Tony as he watched his old teammates practice through a crack in the door?

What kept Tony from apologizing to Coach Harris?

ESSAY

When Lamar says that "every dream has a price," what does he mean? What are some of the sacrifices you may have to make to chase your dream?

Chapter 5: Skippin' Out

What statistic proved to Coach Harris that Tony was more than just a selfish player?

What reasoning did Tony use in trying to persuade Mike not to go to the zoo?

Why is this chapter entitled "Skippin' Out?"

ESSAY

Do you think Tony made the right decision by blocking Coach Harris's path to the locker room? Why or why not?

Chapter 6: Forty- Four

How did Coach Collier raise the stakes of the state championship?

Why did Tony dislike James Thomas?

What is the truest test of a point guard?

ESSAY

In this chapter, Mike struggles to overcome an injury to his knee. He comes back into the game and helps win the state championship. Describe a time in your life when you overcame pain, (physical or emotional), in order to achieve a goal. Was it worth it? Why or why not?

Chapter 7: Invincible

According to Tony, what was the only thing that kept the Hope family from falling apart?

What reason does Mike give Tony for him still being alive?

What seemed important to Tony as he sat in that hospital room?

ESSAY

"Life is a delicate egg, and if you treat it any other way, you'll end up scrambled." Explain this quote using an example in this chapter and an example in your life.

Chapter 8: The Farmer

Who is the "Farmer," and where is he from?

What factors contributed to Tony wanting to leave UNY?

What reasoning did Josh use in trying convince Tony to stay at UNY?

ESSAY

Tony and Josh are from completely different backgrounds, yet they grow to be friends. What did this teach you? Explain using examples from your life. What did Tony and Josh have in common?

Chapter 9: Stepping Into the Light

Why did the Pitbull players smirk when Tony and Josh entered the game?

Who is "Philadelphia's finest?" Where is he from?

What does the chapter title, "Stepping into the Light" mean?

ESSAY

In the first line of this chapter, Tony says, "Mom didn't raise quitters." It would have been easy for Tony to return to Harlem and not face the tough road ahead. What would you have done if you had been in Tony's shoes? Explain.

Chapter 10: From Scratch

Why were Tony and Josh nervous when they heard that there was a new head coach?

Why was Coach Williams smiling after everyone helped Leroy clean the gym?

According to Coach Williams, what does every great player need?

ESSAY

In this chapter, Coach Williams teaches his players the importance of being a team. How does he do this? Cite two examples from this chapter.

Chapter 11: Win-Or-Go-Home

How many points had Tony scored after two years in the championship tournament?

Why did Tony have a hard time recognizing Josh after he came back for his junior year at UNY?

Why did Josh feel a sense of urgency to win the national championship during his junior season?

ESSAY

Until Tony entered the Zone, he said that for "twenty-one years he was the second option." Hard work had prepared Tony for this moment. Was there a time in your life when you stopped relying on others and took control yourself? Describe. What prepared you for your moment?

Chapter 12: Jumping Ship

Why was Tony having a hard time telling Coach Williams that he was leaving for the NBA?

What did Tony realize when he saw Coach come onto the court for their game of one on one?

When "Sweet Feet" is dominating Tony, what memory is conjured up inside him?

ESSAY

In this chapter, we see Tony graduate from college and earn a degree in business. Do you have a subject that you would like to earn a degree in? Why is this your favorite subject? What characteristics do you have that will help you excel in this field?

Chapter 13: Harlem's Hope

Why did Tony put his suntan lotion away?

Why did Tony feel for the kid who was overanxious while defending him?

Why did Mike refuse to watch Tony's game in person? What do you think led him to come anyway?

ESSAY

Congratulations! You have completed another Scobre book. In light of their journey, tell us what you learned from Tony and from Mike. Which of the Hope brothers seems more like you? Of the two, who was more of an inspiration to you? Explain.